Breaking Down the Ca

by Melissa Compton

MEDICAL DISCLAIMER: The information contained in this book is for entertainment purposes only. It is not intended to be a substitute for professional medical advice, diagnosis or treatment. Always seek the advice of your physician or other qualified healthcare provider with any questions you may have regarding a medical condition or treatment and before undertaking a new health care regime, and never disregard professional medical advice or delay in seeking it because of something you have read in this book.

LEGAL DISCLAIMER: The information contained in this book is for entertainment purposes only. It is not intended to be a substitute for professional legal advice or services. Please always consult a qualified legal professional and never disregard legal advice or delay in seeking it because of something you have read in this book.

Chapter 1

Katie looked out of the clear, crystal window of her bedroom in the castle's western tower, at the beautiful, perfect gardens below. She loved the yellow roses that Roy had planted. She especially loved the clock the gardeners had created out of red, yellow, and orange flowers.

She longed for an adventure and, some excitement. She wanted to go somewhere no one knew her, where she could be free and as wild as she wanted without causing a disaster. Her husband Roy had made a fortune working as a Proprietary Trader for a large bank. He had so much money that there wasn't anything he couldn't do or have. He was kind: he had built the castle for her, so she could live a princess fantasy.

When Katie had first seen Roy, she was at the stables tending to her horse. Goliath was a magnificent horse and Katie's very best friend. He was about six feet tall and had a perfect black coat. His mane and tail were so silky and shiny that they reflected the light perfectly. His strength and might was demonstrated by his bulky and muscular build. Katie had thought it was the might and size of Goliath that had caught Roy's attention the day they met.

There were always a few stable hands going about their work. but the stables were quiet that day. Katie was there tending to Goliath. Roy was looking for a new horse to buy, but he quickly forgot about that when he saw Katie.

Katie remembered that day she saw him out of the corner of her eye. She was attracted to his wild curly blond hair and how his eyes sparkled and danced as he smiled at her. He confidently walked over to her and said:

"Hello, I am Roy Kyle."

"Hi, I'm Katie, Katie Maddison."

"That's a magnificent horse, you've got there." Roy said.

“Thank you. His name is Goliath.” Katie replied. She was almost waiting for Roy to launch into an “is he for sale?” speech.

“So, how does a little thing like you, come to own a horse like this?”

“He was a gift from a friend, who owns a ranch in Texas.” Katie said, blushing and looking at the ground, hoping, he wouldn’t see her red cheeks, and then she slowly raised her head.

“A boyfriend?” Roy asked.

“No, her name’s Barbara.” Katie answered, laughing. “You’re a bit forward, aren’t you?”

“I was raised on a policy of if you don’t ask. You don’t get, and I usually get what I go after!” Roy replied.

“Really, and what is it that you want now?” Katie asked.

“Now who’s being forward? I want you to go riding with me.”

"Okay, well how good are you? Because Goliath is quite fast."

"I think, I can keep up." Roy replied, laughing.

"Great! I would love to go riding with you then."

"Good. That would make me very happy. Meet me in the courtyard in 30 minutes."

"Okay! Looking forward to it." Katie said, and smiled as Roy left the stables to get ready.

Katie remembered how drawn she was to him that day. The average man would not have gotten away with being so forward. Well, not without her putting him in his place. But then Roy was far from your average man, a fact he had reminded her of often since. She remembered how excited she had been getting Goliath ready to go. At one-point Katie put his saddle on back to front. Goliath had bucked it off again before she had a chance to try and secure it. Katie said sorry, gave him a hug, and put the saddle on the right way around.

She made her way to the courtyard with Goliath. It was a beautiful day: the sun was high in the sky and golden. And there wasn't a cloud in the sky. Roy entered the courtyard exactly at the minute he had arranged. Katie was impressed he wasn't late. She was only nineteen years old and easily impressed back then.

"Hi, are you ready?"

"Yes, I am ready when you are. Katie."

Roy was riding a lovely chestnut-colored horse; the horse was somewhat slimmer than Goliath, more like a racehorse. It had a lovely shiny coat; Katie noticed it glimmering in the sunshine as they slowly trotted away down a country lane.

"That's a beautiful horse." Katie said.

"Thank you: he's one of mine." Roy said.

"One of yours? How many horses do you have?" Katie asked. Amused and a little confused.

"Oh, I have five more. I came to the stables to buy another. But I haven't yet." Roy said.

"Oh, so do run a stable or farm then?"

"I own a stable for my personal horses, but not as a business." Roy said.

As they continued trotting down a country lane, there was a large wood to the right of them.

"I have an idea. How about a ride through the woods? There's a lovely nature park in the middle with a stream." Katie said.

"Sounds great."

So, they headed off into the woods. Roy was trotting alongside Katie now through the woods, Katie smiled.

Katie loved the woods: it smelled lovely and fresh. And somehow it seemed more private than the open road.

"So, what do you do for a living, if it's not running a stable?" Katie asked.

"I work in finance." Roy said.

"Oh, that sounds boring, are you really smart then?"

Roy laughed out loud. "I try to be."

"Oh, I'm more of a practical person. I don't think I could do a brainy job."

"I think you're very smart indeed."

"Why?"

"Well, you are out riding with me on this lovely day. That was a smart decision."

Katie laughed. "Let's go sit by the stream, brainy boy."

And off they went she couldn't help but notice how well he handled the horse. It seemed obvious that he was a very experienced rider. Roy helped Katie down from Goliath. And they sat by the stream, Goliath was very protective and never left her side.

"Are you Okay Katie?"

"Yes, well I'm a bit hungry. I didn't eat this morning."

"Okay, let's sort that out. How about pizza and salad?" Roy asked.

"That would be great, but we are in the middle of the woods." Katie replied.

"Not a problem."

With that, he walked away and made a phone call,

Katie thought *he's crazy. After all. Who gets pizza delivered into the middle of the woods?*

Roy came back over and sat next to Katie. "It's all sorted. It won't be long." he said.

Yes, crazy! What have I gotten myself into this time?

“I am really glad, you joined me today. You’re a lovely woman.”

“Thank you for inviting me. I am having the best time.”

As they sat there. Katie realized she was drawn in by his eyes. They were beautiful. How could anyone that looked that good, possibly be crazy?

Just then the pizza arrived.

She sat there shocked

“Here you go, Mr. Kyle. If you need anything else, just call.” the delivery man said.

“Thank you very much. I will.” Roy said, handing the man a tip.

As they sat there eating pizza and salad, Katie couldn’t stop staring into Roy’s eyes. She was mesmerized.

“That was amazing.” she said. finishing the last slice of pizza.

“I would have said the pizza was average.”

"No, I mean the way you did that."

Oh, how Katie loved that memory. It was her favorite. And it was just the beginning of their time together. Of course, she had no idea then just how rich and powerful Roy was otherwise it wouldn't have seemed so magical. It all seemed a world away now.

They had so much fun the day they met. It was so innocent and was a break from reality; the rest of her courtship with Roy was a whirlwind of amazing dates. Each one more surprising than the last. Like the time he flew her to Eastbourne in Sussex for dinner. Katie remembered it so well. It was about four weeks into their relationship. They arranged to meet for dinner at 6 pm by a field. At the time, she had thought it was a strange place to meet, but then he had to land that plane somewhere. She remembered standing next to the field and the shock when this small passenger plane landed in the field and how she laughed when Roy had got out and walked towards her and said,

"Ready to go."

"Go where? "Katie replied.

"For dinner." he said.

"Erm, Roy! That's a plane."

"Yes. Katie, it's my plane. And flying is the fastest way to reach Eastbourne."

"So, we're having dinner in Eastbourne?"

"Yes, but you need to get into the plane first, sweetie."

Katie took his hand and followed him to the plane. At this point, she was still thinking he was a little crazy, but it was starting to sink in just how rich he was. They flew to a flight center in between Brighton and Eastbourne on the coast road. Where they transferred to a car with a driver.

You never told me you fly a plane?" Katie said.

"Well, it would be boring if I told you everything at once.

"That is very true."

Suddenly the car was going up a steep incline. Katie moved closer and held on to Roy

"Where exactly is it that we are having dinner?" Katie asked.

"It's at the top of the cliff. The views are great there." Roy answered.

"That explains it."

Roy laughed and held her tight until the car finally came to a stop. When they stepped out of the car, her breath was taken away. There was a restaurant but also fields as far as the eyes could see. There was a sloping view of the entire south downs: it was beautiful. To the other side was a jagged cliff face: it spanned for miles. The sea below was as untamed as the rocks. As they walked towards the restaurant. Katie saw a phone box.

"That seems like an odd place to put a phone box." she said.

"Don't worry about the phone box. Katie. Come on or we will be late." Roy said.

Katie took Roy's hand and went inside the restaurant, where the attendant said.

"Your booth has been prepared to your instructions and is ready, Mr. Kyle."

"Thank you." he said. following her.

When they arrived at the booth. Katie smiled. The booth was in a window corner with a view of the sea. There were big, beautiful, open yellow and cream roses that lined the window. The seats were gold and cream and there was a single white candle on the table. There were large bottles of water on the table. and Roy ordered wine. Katie remembered how she felt like a princess. That night after dinner she said.

"Thank you, Roy. You went to a lot of trouble tonight and it was perfect."

"It's okay. I would do anything to see you smile. You are starting to mean a lot to me." Roy said.

"You're so sweet. I'm very fond of you too." Katie said.

Oh, how perfect things seemed than in the days before they moved to St Just.

Later that night Roy had told Katie how the phone box was connected to a suicide hotline and the cliff was popular with jumpers.

The only night that was better than that was the night he had proposed. It was the night he rented an entire castle. Roy drove Katie out to the countryside: Katie loved old buildings. They had been dating for three months by then, although it still seemed like five minutes because she was having so much fun.

"I've arranged for a night at the castle." Roy said.

"It's not haunted, is it?" Katie asked.

"No, of course not. Anyway, I don't believe in that nonsense."

"I don't have any things."

"Everything you need is in the castle; don't worry."

They made their way inside over the drawbridge.

“Oh, Roy! This is great! You are amazing.” Katie said as she explored the castle. The castle was an unusual triangular shape with 3 towers, a mote surrounding it and a drawbridge leading in, the first room you walked into was the grand hall there was a fireplace and two grand golden and red armchairs at one end of the hall and a long banquet table with dining chairs also red and gold at the other end, there were two staircases leading into the room one was narrow and bare, the other was slightly wider with red carpet if you continued into the grand hall there was a corridor leading out to a small garden surrounded by a private woodland.

“We are having a picnic dinner in the garden. Come on, it’s this way.”

“Okay, lead the way.”

You had to access the garden by walking through the tower. There was a picnic in the middle of the garden. There were lights draping the boundary walls and climbing roses all around. As they got closer. Katie saw everything was decorated pink, her signature color, and there were rose petals scattered everywhere. They sat down on the pink satin blankets laid out.

"This is so perfect." Katie said.

"Thank you; I wanted it to be just right." Roy said.

"A night we could remember proudly forever."

"You remembered it is Valentine's Day then."

"I am aware of it, yes."

"But. Katie, please listen. We've been dating a few months,and I adore you."

Oh my God! He's going to end it.

"Yes, Roy." Katie said.

"I know it's sudden, but all I know is I don't ever want to be without you. So, please Katie Maddison, will you do me the pleasure of becoming my wife." Roy said.

"Yes, of course, yes." Katie shouted. She didn't even think about it.

"You just made me the happiest man alive Katie." he said, leaning in to kiss her.

"We'll go ring shopping in London tomorrow. You can have any ring you desire. In fact, you can have anything."

"I just want you." Katie said.

She was so happy that night. It had been in the days following her engagement that she had told him she wanted a castle like that one, so she could relive that moment forever with him. Katie remembered how easily he'd said, "Sure, I'll commission one for you. You can be my princess." little did she realize it would end up like this.

Now though Roy was always reminding her that with power comes responsibilities. It was usually at that point when Katie would yawn with boredom. Personally, she would rather just give it up and have a simple life and be happy, but that just wasn't an option anywhere in Cornwall at least. She had never understood, why people longed for money and power when it was so restrictive. Rich people had so many rules with society expecting so much from them. Act this way, talk like this and all these people you employ suddenly you are responsible for their lives too and whole families you don't even know relying on you keeping everything exactly as it is.

Katie was bored, fed up, and just wanted to forget all the restrictions. She never did like responsibility; she just wanted to be wild and free like a stallion. The only difference was now she wanted prince charming by her side being just as wild too. She knew Roy just wasn't the type though, as much as she loved him. They had talked about it many times, and she often thought if she could get him somewhere like Texas, maybe the call of country life might take over. Barbara had invited them many times, but Roy always had something requiring his attention, so they couldn't go.

Roy loved his world to be ordered and controlled. It was this attention to detail that had made him so wealthy in the first place.

Chapter 2

Katie stopped staring out the window, like a princess locked in a tower and walked down to the stables. As she walked into the stables, her eyes focused on the row of horses. Katie bumped into Anna, one of the stable girls.

"Good afternoon, Miss Katie." Anna said. Roy insisted that all the staff called her Miss Katie. She thought it sounded strange.

"Good afternoon Anna. Roy's in his study; you can relax."

"Oh, thank God. He's so intense."

Katie laughed. "Oh, he's not that bad."

"So, how's your day going?" Anna asked.

"Boring! To be honest, are any of my horse's ready, to take out? I thought I would take a ride to Penzance away from prying eyes."

"Yes, Katherine is. I won't be a minute."

Anna was one of Katie's only friends on the staff as the rest of them were too busy reporting her every move to Roy.

Katie loved her horse: Katherine, she named her after her grandmother due to the horse's untamable sense of adventure. Katie's grandmother had been a free spirit, she had long red hair and a pale complexion she had so many adventures and Katie loved to hear about them as a child. Katie's grandmother told her how she had once gone horse riding across Mongolia. Katie remembered how Katherine got out of her field once. It had taken four stable hands and a very long rope to get her back. Everyone took the incident in good humor, but Roy pointed out that Katherine might have fallen in the ditch and gotten injured.

Katherine was the first horse Roy had brought Katie as an engagement present. Katie remembered that day well. It was three days after their engagement: Roy was busy planning an engagement party, that Katie couldn't have cared less about, but he had insisted they needed to have one. Katie had gone down to the field to spend some time alone in nature, away from the excitement and panic at the house.

Katie saw Roy walking down to the field with this beautiful horse that was as white as pure snow. It had a blond mane and tail that were planted with pink ribbons as if the horse were going to a show.

“Hi, Roy. What are you up to?” Katie asked as he approached.

“We thought we would come and say hello.”

“That’s a beautiful horse. Whose is it?”

“That’s the thing. She doesn’t have an owner exactly. I thought you might like her.”

“She’s beautiful! I bet she’s fast, too.”

“She’s an engagement present for you because I know you hate the idea of the party.”

“Thank you, you’re so sweet.” Katie said, throwing her arms around Roy.

Roy leaned in and kissed Katie. He loved making her happy.

“I’m going to ride her now.” Katie said.

“Katie, she has no saddle.” Roy shouted as Katie jumped on the horse’s back.

“I don’t need one.” Katie shouted back.

“Well make sure no one sees you. It’s not ladylike.” Roy shouted again.

“You’re so pretty and wild. I am going to call you Katherine.” Katie said to the horse as they raced across the fields. It seemed like such a long time ago as Katie had enjoyed many rides with Katherine since then.

Anna was soon back with a saddled horse. She helped Katie mount Katherine and watched them ride off. As soon as

Anna turned around. Roy was behind her, as if out of nowhere.

“Was that my wife?” Roy asked startling Anna.

“Mr. Kyle, I didn’t see you there. Yes. sir” Anna said.

“Do you know where she is going?”

“No, sir. She never said. She only asked for one of her horses.” Anna replied, stepping backward.

“Well, next time ask.” Roy said. leaning forward and staring hard at her.

“Yes. Sir. Sorry, sir.” Anna blurted out turning away quickly.

With that, Roy stormed off into the castle, and one of the other stable girls comforted Anna.

“I’d love to give him a piece of my mind. He’s just a bully.” Clarice snorted

“Oh, Clarice, you can’t.” Anna said.

“Yeah, yeah, I know.” Clarice laughed as they walked away together.

“What annoys me is he’s such a bully to everyone except princess Katie, of course.” Clarice continued.

“Hey, Katie is nice. It’s not her fault he’s so horrible.” Anna said.

“Yeah, I guess, but she’s not one of us either though. She’s in for a rude awakening when she realizes what he’s really like.” Clarice said.

“Let’s hope she never does.” Anna said.

Meanwhile, Katie was enjoying galloping through the beautiful Cornish landscape. They lived near the edge of the coast in a little village called St Just. Katie loved riding across to Penzance and escaping the watchful eyes of the locals in St Just. She knew they watched everything and reported back. Katie wasn’t a local; she was from Cambridge and proud of it. She felt the disapproving eyes whenever she was out. They were waiting for her to make a mistake. They were so sure of her downfall.

In Penzance, she felt free. She could just relax and be herself. No one cared there who she was. By horse, the journey to Penzance took just over two hours. Katie loved leaving the world behind and just enjoying feeling free. Katie felt free and wild and unstoppable.

About halfway, Katie dismounted from the horse in a field by a stream to stop to rest and give Katherine some water. Katie sat on the grass, the sun was hot and bright, glowing like a fire in the sky. Katie lay down in the long grass, rolling back and forth for fun. Shortly after, they were on their way again. Once in Penzance, Katie sighed with relief. Katie dismounted from Katherine and gave her a big hug and some sugar while she stroked her mane. Katie took the reins and led Katherine on a slow trot around the town. They found a place to rest in Morag park by the fountain. The large fountain was in the centre of the park with cherub statues surrounded by a large area of perfectly smooth green grass. It was a beautiful place to stop on a sunny day, Katie sat next to Katherine on the green grass.

"Oh, Katherine, how I wish we could go on an adventure."

"I love Roy so much, but I know he's way too ordered to be adventurous and spontaneous like me and you." Katie said. Katherine nudged her gently with her nose.

"I'm just so bored and fed up. I feel so controlled by him and not in charge of my own life."

"The only time I am happy is when I'm out, riding, Katherine, and I miss Goliath so much and my friends and family."

"I'm starting to think what on earth have I done. No one understands me. Well, Roy tries sometimes."

"I just wish we could ride away and not come back. But I love him so much. I could never do that." Katie said.

She sat there cuddling Katherine for a while longer, Katie always poured out her troubled heart to Katherine. After all, horses don't argue with people. No one was around so Katie could be honest without worrying about anyone listening to her words. After a while Katie noticed the clouds drawing in and the darkness started to fall like a veil.

"Come on, we'd better head home, before he gets too mad." Katie said.

Chapter 3

Katie remounted Katherine and started heading home. It wasn't long before the sky looked like a black backdrop to the bright moon with its glittering stars. Katie loved being out by moonlight. Now she realized it must be late, so she rode straight home. She was experiencing the calm before the storm: Katie knew Roy would be annoyed. As Katie approached the stables, she saw Roy standing there, face like thunder, with one of the stable boys to the side of him.

"Here we go, Katherine. Good night, lovely." Katie said as she dismounted.

Katie handed her reins to the stable boy who took Katherine to her stall.

"Have you, any idea what time it is. Katie Kyle?" Roy demanded.

"Well." Katie replied like a cheeky teenager, glancing at her watch.

"And it's Katie Maddison- Kyle actually." She added before Roy could answer.

"It was not a question. Katie-pain-in-the-neck-Maddison-Kyle. This must stop. You cannot just disappear without telling anyone where you are going." Roy shouted back.

Katie sighed.

"Are you my husband or my jailer?" Katie yelled.

"Both, when needed." Roy roared.

"I am your husband, and you belong to me, kindly behave accordingly."

The anger was showing on his face now, he looked like he was going to explode but Katie was too angry to stop and laugh.

"I belong to no one, but myself, and I will act as I see fit." Katie roared back.

As Katie stood there waiting for a response, Roy took a step towards her and, with a huge swooping action slapped Katie so hard he knocked her head to the side. Katie felt Roy's hand strike her face; there was a massive clap and then a stinging sensation in her cheek.

"I will never forgive you for that! Never come near me again." Katie demanded as she turned away.

"Katie, I didn't mean that" Roy shouted, but he knew it fell on deaf ears.

Katie ran into the castle and locked herself away in her dressing room. She could hear Roy running, shouting, and screaming her name down the corridor. But she was safe in the dressing room. She went into the bathroom in her dressing room and put some icy water on her cheek; a bruise was beginning to form. She was still in shock no idea what she was doing or what she was going to do. Katie put on a pink fluffy dressing gown it was huge and always made her feel comforted instantly. She curled up on a rug and started to cry. In this room, she felt safe. It was the only room in the castle only Katie had a key to, and the locks were strong, strong enough to keep anyone out. So, she was not leaving. Katie curled up on the large pink and silver fluffy rug lying on the sparkling black tiles and started to cry, she must have cried on that rug all night.

Chapter 4

Meanwhile, Roy was drinking in his study; he paced back and forth as he threw the last of the whiskey onto the flames of the open fire and watched the flames roar. Out in the courtyard, Roy's friend Michael appeared.

"Hi, Michael." Anna said.

"Hello, Anna, you're working late." Michael said.

"I'm just leaving."

"Do you know where Roy is?"

"He's in his study, Michael."

"Thank you. Anna." Michael said, walking toward the entrance of the house.

"Bye. Michael." Anna said as she left the courtyard.

Michael walked straight to Roy's study.

"Hey Roy." Michael said.

“Michael, I’m glad to see you.” Roy said.

“Yeah, so was your annoying little stable hand.”

“Yeah, Anna’s got a little crush on you, but I have bigger problems right now.”

“What am I going to do with her?”

“Why? What’s she done now? We are talking about Katie?”

“Yes, Katie. It’s always Katie, she’s so wild and careless. We had an agrument because she was out on her own again.”

“I told when you married her. You can’t control a girl like that. It’s like trying to hold and contain a cyclone.”

“I lost my temper, she is hiding somewhere, the question is how I fix this, and I know you’re right about controlling her.” Roy said.

“Oh Roy, you put her in a world she doesn’t understand, and your temper got the better of you. I do have an idea though.”

“Well, I could certainly use the help..”

"This friend in Texas, what's her name, doesn't she keep inviting her over? What about setting up a surprise and sending her there for a few days. Katie can calm down and will think it's sweet of you. Meanwhile, she's out of view and can't embarrass you further, and when she returns, she will be more grounded."

"Michael, that's inspired! I knew there was a reason I keep you around."

" Thanks."

"Let's have a drink."

"Great."

Michael stayed for a few drinks with Roy. They talked about when things were so much simpler before Roy married Katie. They laughed and laughed. When Michael finally left Roy decided to get to work on his plan to send Katie to Texas.

Roy poured another glass of whiskey and sat at his desk ready to call Barbara. He was thinking about what to say. He couldn't tell her the truth, but maybe he could give her the highlights. He flicked through his address book until he found her number.

He slowly dialed the long number

"Hello." Barbara answered.

"Hi, Barbara. It's Roy." he said.

"Is everything ok?" Barbara asked, it was unusual for Roy to call and not Katie.

"Yes. I was wondering if you'd help with something for Katie."

"Ok. I'm all ears."

"Katie has been feeling low. She's fed up, I guess. She doesn't really have many friends here, so, I was thinking a surprise trip to Texas to see you might cheer her up."

"That's a lovely idea. I'm always here for Katie. She knows that"

"Great! Yes, she told me what a good friend you are. I think she misses Goliath too. I know she has Katherine, but it's not the same. He was her first horse and everything."

"So, when are you thinking of?"

"Is tomorrow too soon?"

"No, the sooner the better. Don't worry; I'll get to the bottom of what's troubling her."

"Thank you. I'll make the arrangements and text you the details, so you can meet her at the airport.."

"Okay. You take care now." Barbara said, before ending the call.

Roy wasn't too convinced about Barbara's claim to get to the bottom of things. But he had little options available to him right now. So, he got to work. Roy worked all night, booking flights and transferring money into an account Katie could access in Texas and arranging a car to take them to the airport. When he was done, he sat back and finished his whiskey, then went to bed to get a few hours' sleep.

Chapter 5

When Roy woke up the following morning, he showered and changed. Then he went to the study to print out all the tickets and information for Katie's trip. He said to the maid:

"I want to take breakfast in the dining room. Kindly find my wife and ask her to join me."

"Yes. Sir. right away." said the maid and she was gone again.

Roy gathered the documents and made his way to the dining room.

The maid knew exactly where to find Katie. Everyone knew if she was missing, she was in her dressing room.

The maid knocked on the dressing room door three times loudly.

"Yes, can I help you?" Katie said.

"Mr. Kyle is requesting you join him for breakfast in the dining room."

“Is he now! And what kind of mood is Mr. Kyle in this morning?”

“Miss Katie, he’s in his usual mood.”

“Very well. You may tell Mr. Kyle that I will attend.”

“Thank you, miss.” the maid replied as she left. It was an unusual way for Katie to answer but all the staff was aware of the fight the night before and therefore, was very cautious that day.

Katie showered, changed, and headed to the dining room. Roy was waiting for her. The bruise on her face was still visible, although she was trying her best to hide it with her hair.

Katie stood at the entrance to the dining room and for once she was grateful for the large dining table and seating Roy had insisted, they put in there. It was a long oak table with oak and dusky pink chairs ten of them in fact. Katie never understood why they needed that many. Roy was seated at the head of the table, and Katie stood at the foot of it. So much space divided them, and this made Katie feel safe enough to stand her ground this morning.

“Katie, I am so sorry I hit you. There’s no excuse. Honestly, I’ve been worried all night. Are you ok?” Roy asked.

“What’s this all about?” Katie demanded.

“I have a surprise for you.”

“I’m not certain I can stand any more of your surprises.”

“It’s a pleasant one. I promise.”

“ Really. I am not sure you know what pleasant is!”

“Katie, what do you mean by that?”

“Never mind what is it?”

“I wanted to do something nice for you. So, I arranged for you to visit Barbara in Texas. Your flight leaves at three this afternoon!” Roy continued, pushing the flight documents onto the table.

"Did you tell Barbara, what you did?"

"No. I did not."

"Well, that's something at least." Katie replied. She wanted to explain to Barbara herself. She was embarrassed and hurt that she could love a man who would just hit her like that. And wasn't sure her friend would understand.

"I can't help but wonder if this is, a sweet treat for me or a way to get me out of the way for a while to hide your handy work!"

Roy left the room using the opposite side of the room of Katie, so their paths didn't cross. Katie walked to the top of the table and collected the flight documents.

Katie was secretly relieved to be going to Texas. If she had thought of it, she would have gone last night. But she knew her husband wasn't doing this out of the kindness of his heart. In fact, Katie wasn't even sure he had one. She wasn't sure if she would want to return, after all, Texas would give her the freedom she had been craving. Katie made her way back to the dressing room to pack.

Katie loved her dressing room. It was the one place in the castle that was truly hers, full of only her things. She had designed the dressing room herself, too, which was probably why it didn't feel like the rest of the castle. Katie could lock the world out and enjoy the peace and did quite often. Katie packed for her trip and sat on the pink and pine seat in the dressing room until it was time to leave.

There was another knock at the door.

"Mr. Kyle says it's time to leave, Miss Katie." the maid said.

"Very well. I will be there in a minute." Katie replied.

Katie opened the door with a suitcase in one hand and flight tickets in the other. She made her way slowly downstairs where Roy was waiting. He extended his hand out as she walked off the bottom step. Katie accepted it as there were people around; she could hear them whispering about the bruise on her face from the night before. It had been impossible to hide as they made their way to the car outside. Katie suddenly broke away and ran to the stables to see Katherine.

Katie hugged Katherine as tight as she could.

“I’m going away for a little while Katherine. I’ll miss you, dear friend.” Katie whispered.

“Katie, we really need to go.” a voice from behind said. Katie returned to the car and got into the back seat before, they left for the airport.

Chapter 6

Katie was sitting, and Roy was chatting on about something or other. Katie wasn't really paying any attention; she just wanted to be away from him. Roy reached out to touch her arm, but Katie flinched and edged away from him.

"I am so sorry, Katie." Roy said.

"I need time to heal." Katie said.

"Take all the time you need."

"Thank you." Katie said. She put in her earphones to listen to music and turned away to face the window. After a long drive, they were finally at the airport. After Katie was all checked in, Roy said.

"I put some money in your account, so you can access it in Texas. There's plenty there, but if you run low, just give me a call."

"Thank you. I'm sure it'll be fine." Katie said.

"Can you call me when you get there to let me know you got there safely. I'll worry."

"Yes, I will."

"I love you so much. I am really going to miss you. We've never really been apart."

"It's probably about time, we had a break when you think about it."

"Bye Katie. Have a safe flight!"

"Goodbye, Roy." Katie said as she turned away and headed for her flight lounge. It was a little early, but Katie didn't care; she couldn't take any more of the awkwardness between them. She never looked back.

Katie sat in the airport departure lounge, reading a book. It was all about horse care. She was glad Barbara was meeting her at Houston. The time flew, and soon Katie turned off her phone, put her book away, and boarded her flight. She was pleased to have a window seat; it helped her not to panic during take-off. She was relieved now and quite tired; she put the blanket that was in her flight pack around her, snuggled into the side of her seat, and began drifting off.

When Katie awoke, they were landing in Houston. The landing process, getting off the plane, and clearing customs seemed to last forever. Katie was relieved when she finally made it to the entrance hall and could see Barbara waving and speed walking towards her. Barbara threw her arms around Katie

"Barbara, it's good to see you." Katie said.

"Yes, it's been too long." Barbara said.

"Indeed."

"It seems we have some catching up to do!" Barbara said staring at the bruise on Katie's face.

"Oh, yes."

"Don't worry; I have something at the house that will clear that up."

Katie smiled back, and they were soon on their way, driving through Texas in Barbara's car. Barbara's ranch was called Happy Acre's and was in a town called Fort Kellna just outside of Houston.

As they were driving up the long driveway to the ranch, Katie spotted Goliath with a worker in the field.

"Do you mind, if I go and say hello?" Katie asked.

"To Goliath or Joshua?" Barbara teased.

"Ha-ha! Joshua is cute though." Katie laughed.

"Yeah, I quite often wonder how he gets in jeans that tight though." Barbara said.

"Barbara!"

Barbara pulled over and shouted.

“Joshua, this is Katie. She is going to spend some time with Goliath.”

“Ok, Barbara.” Joshua replied.

Katie jumped out of the car and climbed the fence. Joshua helped her down.

“Hello, Katie.” he said.

“Hey, so how’s my horse?”

“He’s yours, is he?”

“Yes, he was a gift. He’s the best horse in the world.”

“Yeah, for sure.” Joshua said, looking at Katie. He was trying to figure out why he was so captured by her.

“He’s good.”

“Hey, boy.” Katie said as she stroked Goliath and hugged his neck.

“I have missed you, old friend.”

Goliath used to be on a farm in Georgia; that's where Barbara had brought him. Goliath's party trick was to buck riders to the floor without warning. Being dropped from a horse of that size and strength almost always led to injuries, usually a broken something or other, thus making him very unpopular with ranch staff. Katie was sitting on the grass next to Goliath.

"It's so good to see you, Goliath. It's not the same without you."

"We'll take lots of rides and walks while I'm here and lots time together."

"So, much has happened since I saw you last." Katie said

"Joshua, I am going to ride him back." Katie shouted.

"Ride? Goliath hasn't a saddle, Katie." Joshua replied. He was worried that Barbara wouldn't be happy if Katie got hurt riding Goliath before she had even settled in.

"I don't need a saddle. Can you keep up with us?" Katie asked, throwing her hair back.

"Yeah, I can keep up." Joshua sighed; he really wasn't sure about this, but he could see Katie had no plans of taking "no" for an answer.

Why were the pretty ones always trouble?

Katie climbed onto Goliath's back while he was lying down in the grass. She leaned forward and whispered.

"Come on, boy. Let's go home slowly so Joshua can keep up."

Goliath slowly rose to his hooves as Katie held on to his neck. Katie looked down at Joshua.

"You ready then?" She laughed.

"Yeah, I'm always ready." Joshua replied.

Goliath slowly trotted off towards the house and the stables; Katie looked behind and saw Joshua slowly walking behind. She slowed to a halt.

"Are we going too fast?" she asked.

"No, I'm just giving you room in case he bucks you to the floor."

"Don't worry; Goliath loves me. He's always good for me."

Katie and Goliath started trotting on again and they were soon back at the stables. Katie took Goliath in and settled him in his stall.

"Goodnight, Goliath." she said as she walked out of the stall.

"Bye Joshua." Katie shouted as she waved and headed for the house.

"Bye Katie." he shouted back.

Chapter Seven

"There you are." Barbara said.

"Yeah, sorry. Was I a long time?" Katie asked.

"It's all right. I just thought you might be hungry." Barbara said.

Katie spotted the lunch on the table.

"I am! Thank you; it looks great." Katie said, moving towards the table.

Katie sat at the table with Barbara, both munching away at the finger food buffet on the table. Barbara poured them a cup of tea, just as Katie was finishing her last mouthful of food.

"Now, are you going to tell me what's going on?" Barbara asked.

"I guess I owe you an explanation." Katie replied.

"I'll say you do."

"So, what did Roy tell you?"

"That you were feeling down and needed a break." Barbara.

"I thought it odd because it didn't sound like you."

"He said what?" Katie sighed and rolled her eyes.

"I guess, it's partly true. I have been feeling trapped; everything is so controlled."

"Go on."

"Well, it's another world there in Cornwall. Everything is ordered and only authorized by Roy, I have been feeling like I was trapped in a prison. Not that Roy would notice, he's always busy in his study and only Michael, his friend is allowed in there."

"Katie, I wish you'd called."

"I mean he built that castle. It supposed to be a dream come true. Instead, it's a fortress. I have no freedom; only by riding down to the coast can I be myself. He's always telling me that money brings power and responsibility. To be honest, I'd rather give it all up." Katie said, stopping for a sip of tea.

"Maybe I am ungrateful; I don't know. So, I took my horse. Katherine out unannounced. I am supposed to announce every little thing. We went to the coast; it's a long ride so it was late when I got back. Roy was waiting. He was so angry; he kept going on about how I belonged to him and needed to behave myself, so we argued. Then, out of nowhere, he hit me. It's the first time he's ever done that. I locked myself in my dressing room; it's the only room only I have a key to."

"I don't think you're selfish at all, Katie. It sounds awful; I didn't know Roy was like that." Barbara said.

"Neither did I. he treats me like a possession, and thinks I shouldn't have a mind of my own."

Barbara brushed Katie's hair back and put cream on her bruise.

"It's Arnica cream. It will help the bruise. Only time can help your fear of him. But I am happy that you are here and safe."

"Thank you. It's good to be here."

"I have planned a pamper evening, just me and you this evening." Barbara said.

"Ooh with wine?"

"Of course, you can't have a night in without wine." Barbara answered and they both laughed.

"I've missed girly time so much. I don't really have friends in Cornwall. Everyone there just reports back to Roy, and I can't be bothered with it." Katie said.

"Well, you don't have to worry about that here."

"Oh, I was supposed to call Roy when I arrived. I better get it over with." Katie said, taking out her phone and walking into the Kitchen.

"Hello, Roy! Sorry, I forgot to call." Katie said.

"Katie, I will talk to you tomorrow. It's late here. Try calling at a reasonable hour." Roy demanded.

"Yes, Roy, ok." Katie said before putting the phone away.

Katie turned towards Barbara and smiled.

"It pains me to see you so controlled, you used to have such a free spirit. What happened?" Barbara asked.

"Life changed. I guess, and I had to change with it. it's not all bad; he just hates his world being out of order and control. Roy owns and controls an entire village in Cornwall. It's what he's used to." Katie said.

"It's such a different world from what I know." Barbara said.

Later that evening, they headed upstairs to a large bathroom suite. As Katie walked in, she was amazed. The room was huge, the size of a large bedroom. There was a walk-in shower and sauna that you could sit in, and the bath was a jacuzzi. Everything was white and gold, even the towels. There was even a sofa! Candles were everywhere. White sparkling tiles with gold leaves printed on them were on the floor.

"This is amazing." Katie said.

"Thanks. I love it." Barbara replied.

Katie made herself comfortable on the sofa while Barbara was gathering bath oils, face packs, lotions for her pamper session and some wine.

Barbara poured them both a glass of wine while Katie was still curled up on the sofa.

"Do you remember that time, I accidentally rode your brother's motorcycle around the car park and couldn't stop?" Katie asked.

"Oh yes, you were only eight, and he left you sitting on it with the keys in while he opened the garage door." Barbara said.

"It was so funny watching him try to catch you to stop the bike because you didn't know how."

"I didn't know how I had started it in the first place, let alone how to stop it."

"That was a funny day! That bike was so fast."

"Don't know what made me think of that." Katie said.

"Oh, do you remember the first time we went to a shooting range?" Barbara asked.

"You beat everyone at target practice, and you had never held a gun. My brother Andrew was so jealous."

"I know! People were talking. I was just like what did I do?" Katie laughed.

"We've had some amazing memories."

"Yes, and plenty more to make."

"Let's get started with these foot soaks." Barbara said.

"Yeah, now that feels good." Katie replied, putting her feet in the bowl.

They spent the night, pampering themselves, giggling, and drinking wine. Barbara was happy to see Katie relaxed.

Katie fell asleep on the sofa, so Barbara helped her to her room, Katie just looked up and giggled.

“Ooh purple, I love purple! It goes so well with pink.” Katie said and fell on the bed and went to sleep.

Chapter 8

“Good morning, Joshua.” Barbara said the following morning.

“Good morning, Barbara. Just wondering if there’s anything important you need me to do today.” Joshua answered.

“Well, I’m having a party for Katie tonight. Everyone’s invited, so there are caterers, a tent, decorators, and music. I am going to set up the bottom field. Now, Katie doesn’t know so make sure everyone knows to distract her from the field until tonight. Apart from that it's business as usual” Barbara said, smiling.

“Ok, I’ll take care of it.” Joshua replied.

“Great, I have to pop out and pick a few things up. I’ll be back by lunch.” Barbara said, grabbing her keys and heading for the front door.

“See you later.” Joshua shouted.

It was later that morning when Katie woke up. She showered and got ready to go downstairs. There was a note on the dining table with a tray of pancakes, fruit, maple syrup and a pot of coffee. It read:

Morning Katie,

I have a few things to sort out but make yourself at home, and Joshua is around if you need anything. I will be back by 2 pm at the latest.

Love Barbara xx

Katie poured herself a cup of coffee and began eating some breakfast. She just loved how quiet the house was. It was nice to eat without someone hovering around you or watching your every move. Katie liked how fresh the fruit was in America. Why couldn't it be like that in England? That reminded her that she had to call Roy. Katie wondered what his mood would be like this morning. It was best to call him and get it done.

Katie began dialing his number, luckily for her Roy was in a much better mood:

“Morning Roy.” Katie said.

“Katie! Hey, I wasn’t sure you’d call after the way I treated you yesterday. I am so sorry. I was just tired.” Roy said.

“I thought I should call, that word ‘sorry,’ seems to be coming up a lot lately.”

“I know, but I really am. I miss you so much. It’s strange here without you.”

Katie paused before answering, there was a moment’s awkward silence.

“Yes, I’m sure.”

“Anyway, I am going to go. I just wanted to call and say hello.” Katie continued.

“Okay, I love you.” Roy said.

“I know.” Katie said before hanging up.

Well, at least he was polite today.

Katie's thoughts changed to what she wanted to do with the day until Barbara returned. She decided to just go explore, so she put her walking shoes on. Katie walked outside the sun was blazing down and the horses were out in the fields. There was staff running around, some were carrying boxes of ribbons and glasses, some were walking with horses.

"Hello Katie." the people said.

"Hello." Katie said.

She wondered what was going on; it was very busy. Katie thought there may be a horse show of some sort. Katie walked down to a huge fenced-in field. There were no horses in, but there was a catering truck and a tent. There was also a tent filled with balloons. Suddenly Katie heard a voice behind her:

"Katie, you can't be here. It's for a private function later."

"Oh, can't I now? I want to explore."

"Let's go find somewhere else to explore, shall we? Did you get bored?" Joshua asked, leading Katie away.

"I'm not a child, but, yes, I'm bored" Katie answered.

"Where are you taking me?"

"To see the horses. Maybe the ponies if you can behave for five minutes." Joshua teased.

"You sound like my father." Katie said.

They continued walking until they came to a field with Goliath and a few of the larger horses in it. Katie gave Goliath a hug and said,

"Hello boy, sorry I got stuck with annoying Joshua today."

"Is that right" Joshua said as he walked past towards the horse behind Goliath shaking his head.

"Let's go riding." Joshua said.

"Hey, Bryan can you saddle up Goliath and Moses for me? We're going out for a ride."

“Are you sure, you want to take Goliath?” Bryan asked.

“Yeah, it’s her I am not sure about.” Joshua said.

Katie stood there sticking her tongue out him.

“Nice, very ladylike.” Joshua said.

“You think you’re so smart, but it’s all talk.” Katie said.

Katie started laughing, brushing her hair back; it was blowing in the wind. She sat on a fence, waiting for the horses to come back. It wasn’t long before the horses were ready. Joshua helped Katie onto Goliath; she smiled and said thank you. Before Joshua could turn around, she was riding out of the field on Goliath, and this time she wasn’t going slowly.

“Katie, you don’t know where you are going.” Joshua said.

Bryan laughed.

“She’s a pain; I’m telling you Bryan.” Joshua said.

“I guess you better catch up fast then.” Katie yelled back.

As it was, she knew exactly where she was going. Katie spent every summer in Texas as a teenager. staying with family friends in Houston. Katie knew Joshua thought she was just some city girl from England. She had lived in the city once; it didn't last long Katie loved the simpler life.

"I'm going to have to keep an eye on you." Joshua said.

Katie laughed and turned down an old, dirt track to the north of the ranch. Joshua was surprised Katie knew her way around so well, but he was relieved that she was at least going at a reasonable pace now.

"You're actually, not a bad rider." Joshua said.

"Thanks, it's pretty much all I have ever wanted to do." Katie said.

"I've always worked on the ranch."

"There's a little stream, just past the next bend. Let's stop there."

"Okay."

Once they were by the stream. Joshua helped Katie dismount from Goliath, and they sat by the stream.

"There's something relaxing about sitting by the water, don't you think?" Katie said.

"It's one of my favorite things to do." Joshua said.

"Me too, but I don't often get the chance at home."

"Must be hard. How come you know your way around so well?"

"I spent a lot of time in Houston and around here as a teenager."

"Ah, that makes sense."

"We better head back, I don't want to miss Barbara."

"Yes, I suppose I will have to do some work today."

They remounted the horses and headed back to the stables. When they arrived, Katie said.

“Thank you, for taking me riding. It was nice to have company.”

“Anytime.” Joshua said.

Katie made her way back up to the house. When Katie walked into the room, Barbara was waiting for her.

“My lord, you got country real fast.” Barbara said.

“Hey, Barbara. What? Katie asked.

“Little shorts and T-shirt?”

“I do live in the country, you know.”

“Calm down, I’m just playing, Bryan told me you and Joshua went riding.”

Katie just laughed. They sat down and had a cup of tea.

Katie had just finished her tea and was relaxing on the sofa when Barbara said.

“I’ve thought we could go out for dinner tonight.”

“Okay, sounds good.” Katie said.

It had been so long since Katie had a good friend she could relax and spend time with that spending time with Barbara just doing everyday things like going out to dinner, seemed wonderful to her.

“I have missed having someone to talk to and trust without being judged.” Katie said.

“Is it that bad there?”

“It takes years for a new person to be accepted in St. Just. It’s lonely, and I think because I married Roy and I’m not rich like him. I’ll never be accepted.”

“People here are really friendly. Just concentrate on having fun..”

“Thanks! It’s great to be around people that don’t take everything so seriously. I really need to just have fun and enjoy life again.”

Chapter 9

They both went upstairs to pick out outfits for the evening. Barbara was surprised at how down-to-earth, but beautiful Katie's outfits were. She had expected Katie's taste in clothes to be more formal; she wasn't sure Katie had anything suitable for sitting in a field all night. Katie had the perfect outfit though; it was an ankle-length, royal blue dress with white lace trim. She also had a silk wrap to keep her arms warm. She topped the outfit with little, white cowboy boots. As Katie pulled the outfit from the wardrobe in her room. She said,

"I am going to wear this."

Barbara knew she was going to look stunning. Barbara decided to wear a strappy, light blue dress and a white crochet wrap. Katie went off to spend an hour in the jacuzzi bath; she was excited to try it out. Barbara left to make sure all the arrangements and the work was done.

Katie went into the bathroom and locked the door. She filled the bath, turned on the Jacuzzi, slipped in and relaxed. It was heaven; it just what she had needed at that moment. She played with the bubbles, blowing handfuls of them into the air. While she was singing, she kicked her legs up in the air. When Barbara returned, Katie was still in the bath.

Barbara headed upstairs and knocked on the door.

"You okay in there, Katie? It's 6 pm." Barbara said.

"Yes, I'm fine. I am going to get ready now." Katie said.

"Me too. See you in a minute." Barbara said, disappearing into her room.

By the time, Katie passed Barbara's room on the way to her own room, Barbara was already dressed.

"You look beautiful." Katie said.

"Thank you."

It wasn't long before Katie was ready to go too. She headed downstairs feeling very confident and beautiful. Joshua was standing in the hall with Barbara. Katie could see him as she came down the stairs.

"Wow, you look stunning." Barbara said.

"Yes, she does." Joshua said.

"Thank you! Hi, Joshua." Katie said.

"Hi, Katie! Are you two, ready to go?" Joshua asked.

"Yes." they both answered.

"So, where are we going?" Katie asked.

"You will see when we get there." Barbara said.

All three of them made their way down to the field where the barbeque was. As they got to the field, there was pink ribbon and lace draped over anything that stood still, and they observed a "Welcome, Katie" banner hanging over the fence. The catering truck was cooking, burgers, sausages, and every kind of meat you could imagine. There was music playing; the tent was now a drink tent full of people. There were people everywhere; Katie had never seen so many people in one place. There was a tent full of pink and pearl white balloons. Thankfully there were few people in the balloon tent.

At least there is one place I can go to escape the crowd, now just how to get over to the balloon tent politely.

She turned to Barbara.

"This is great! Thank you."

"You're welcome sweetie."

"You know a lot of people."

"Yes, I think everyone in town is here."

"And you remembered pink is my signature color."

"Of course, I would never forget your favorite things."

Katie saw Bryan walking towards her.

"Hello Katie." said Bryan.

"Hello Bryan."

A tall thin man in his late 40's with brown hair wearing trousers a shirt and a tie was approaching Katie.

"Hello Katie. I'm John MacAulay. I'm the police chief in town. Come and meet my wife and daughters."

"Hello, Mr. MacAulay. I would love to."

Katie politely followed the man to the middle of the field.

"Hello Katie." a trio of women said.

"Katie, this is my wife, Susie, and our daughters, Lynette and Cordy."

Susie stepped forward she had long blonde wavy hair was quite slim and was in her late forty's. Lynette was on her left with short light brown hair and blue eyes and medium build and a friendly smile. Cordy was on her right she had long brown hair, big blue eyes she was about the same build as Lynette and the same age somewhere around twenty-five.

“Hello.” replied Katie. She looked around she was trying to work out how to avoid the crowd that seemed to be surrounding her. She never dealt with crowds well and was beginning to get overwhelmed. She couldn’t see Barbara or Joshua anymore.

There was a sudden onset of voices.

“Hello, Katie. How are you?”

Katie wasn’t sure who had said what, she felt like she was spinning round fast and couldn’t stop.

“Excuse me, just a minute.” Katie said. She sat on the grass in the balloon tent with balloons all around her and breathed a sigh of relief to have some space to herself. Then there was a voice:

“Katie, what are you doing?”

Katie turned around to see Bryan stood behind her.

“Taking a break. I was struggling with all those people all saying hello at once, and they kept getting closer. At one point, I thought they were going to swallow me whole.”

Bryan laughed. “Let me guess; you don’t share Barbara’s love of crowds.”

“No, I thought if I sat down here, I could rest for a while. Please don’t tell Barbara; she’d be upset.”

“I won’t. Do you want a drink or something while you’re resting down there?”

“You know, a drink would be lovely.”

“I’ll be back in a minute.”

“Thank you, Bryan.”

Bryan walked off towards the tent. Joshua was walking towards the tent from the other direction. He walked straight up to Bryan, looking around as he did.

“Hi Bryan. Have you seen Katie? She’s disappeared.” Joshua said.

“Yeah, found her hiding in the balloon tent. It’s all a bit much for her. I am just getting her a drink.”

“It’s okay. I will take her a drink.”

“Thanks, Joshua.”

Joshua went off to find Katie, with the drink in one hand and a hotdog in the other. He found her sitting with her legs crossed on the grass under a group of balloons.

“Joshua, is that drink for me?”

“Yes, it is. It's fruit punch. Are you okay Katie?”

“Yes, I just needed a break from the crowd.”

“Is that hot dog for me, too?”

“You can have it.”

“Great.”

"If you can bear to tear yourself away from all the attention, I would like to show you something."

"I think, I can manage that."

Katie took a bite of the hot dog and stood up. She walked by Joshua's side as he led her through the crowd.

People were shouting "hello" at Katie as they walked through.

She shouted hello back but kept walking.

"Don't make eye contact." Joshua said

Katie didn't and once they had cleared the field. He said,

"And that's how you lose a crowd politely in Fort Kellna."

"Thank you. I will have to remember that. So where are we going?"

"You'll see when we get there."

Katie followed Joshua, eating the hot dog and taking sips of her drink along the way.

Chapter 10

Joshua led Katie to a cliffside behind the ranch that overlooked everything for miles. He put his jacket down for Katie to sit on and sat next to her.

“Oh my, you can see everything from up here. Everything looks so small.”

“I love it up here; it’s so peaceful, and no one comes up here that often.”

“Yes, it’s lovely and quiet.”

“Being nosey is a national pastime in Fort Kellna, so it’s good to be able to get away from all that.”

“It’s pretty, too. The ranch looks like a little valley from up here. It reminds me of under mountain road in Connecticut.”

“I’ve never left Fort Kellna; it’s all I know..”

“I always wondered what it would be like to only know one place my whole life; my family traveled a lot..”

"I think it makes people closer when you live somewhere, and people aren't leaving all the time. The downside is we don't get many new people here so when we do, it turns into a bit of a circus.."

"Yes, I noticed.."

Katie and Joshua sat there, looking at the view below them, in silence. Joshua gently reached for Katie's hand, not sure how she would react, but Katie just let him hold her hand and smiled.

"I better get back. Barbara will kill me if I miss my own party." Katie said.

"Ok, let's go.."

Joshua walked Katie back down into the party, and then disappeared into the crowd.

Katie spotted Cordy walking towards her. Cordy had a bright yellow dress on which was hard to miss but went well, with her long brown hair and blue eyes.

"Hello, Katie.."

"Hello, Cordy.."

"So how long are you visiting the town for?"

"I'm not sure yet.."

"Is it a scandal? How I love scandals!"

"No, I'm just visiting Barbara. She's an old friend.."

"Well, maybe I will see you again while you're here.."

"Yeah, maybe.."

Barbara walked over after Cordy had left.

"I thought you had left us for the night.."

"It was a bit busy, so I took a walk.."

"It's ok. There's nothing that happens on this ranch I don't know about. It's my job. You don't have to hide your friendship with Joshua from me. I'm glad you're making friends.."

"Thank you. I am so used to being judged it might take me a while to adjust.."

Katie glanced toward a clearing in the crowd where she saw Joshua chatting with some friends. Then she saw Cordy, walking up to Cordy she said,

"Cordy, come dance with me.."

"Okay, just let me get Lynette.."

Cordy walked towards Lynette. Lynette was standing there brushing her brown hair to the side she had a light blue shift dress on. It brought out the blue of her eyes. She smiled as Cordy approached.

"Lynette, come here."

"Just a minute." Lynette said.

Katie started dancing with Lynette and Cordy. Joshua spotted her and, with some of his friends came over to join in. Katie was having a blast showing off her fancy footwork;

she danced so much she got dizzy, and she nearly fell over. Joshua caught her and sat her down.

“Are you all right?”

“Yes, I think I have had enough dancing for now..”

“Good call..”

Katie went over to sit by Barbara.

“Hey, Barbara..”

“Hi, Katie. Are you having fun?”

“Yes, I just need a rest after too much dancing..”

“You always did love to dance..”

Katie couldn’t help but watch Joshua out of the corner of her eye.

What am I doing? I need to get a grip on this! I am still married, and Roy is expecting me home any day.

“You look tired Katie.” Barbara said.

"Yes, I am a bit.."

"Joshua, can you take Katie back to the house for me?"

"Yeah sure, Barbara.."

"I won't be long; people are starting to leave.."

"Don't worry, I'll be fine." Katie said.

Katie and Joshua started to walk towards the house.

"Come on Katie.."

"You're so bossy and sure of yourself.."

"Are you drunk?"

"Maybe."

Katie stopped in the middle of the path and sat down.

"What now?" Joshua asked.

"I am going to sit here and not move.."

"Why?"

“Why not? I can because I’m a princess..”

“You're a little, nuts..”

“Seriously, I have the castle and everything..”

“And the prince?”

“Well, he used to be..”

“Come on, Katie. Let’s get you inside..”

“No, I am staying here..”

Joshua was getting bored now, so he just picked Katie up, put her over his shoulder and started walking towards the house.

“Joshua put me down at once.” Katie demanded.

Joshua just ignored her. He wanted to get Katie into the house and go home. As he walked into the entrance of the house, he put Katie down.

“Ooh you.” Katie said.

"Yes, what about me?"

"You are so infuriating.."

"You're so drunk. Now you are safely in the house, I'm going.."

Joshua left, and Katie just sat there until Barbara came in.

"Hi Katie, are you, all right?"

"Just tired, you don't mind if I go straight to bed, do you?"

"Of course not.."

"I think that wine went straight to my head.."

"I'll see you in the morning.."

"Good night. Barbara and thank you for tonight. It was great.."

"Good night. Katie.."

Katie went up to bed. She felt dizzy, a little guilty, a bit angry, and a lot happy.

How dare Joshua have handled me like I was a sack of potatoes. On the other hand, I loved how strong he was. Oh God, I've got to call Roy. Better to get it over with.

Katie took out her phone and dialed Roy's number. She wasn't even aware of what time it was, but she was supposed to call him at 3 p.m. each day.

"Hello Roy.."

"Katie it's late. Why would you call me now?"

"Because I don't know what time it is."

"It's too late to be calling anyone."

"Really."

"You need to stop behaving like a spoilt child and come home."

Katie slammed the phone down.

Why do men think they can order me around like a servant?

Barbara was downstairs sat on the sofa with her feet up having a cup of tea. She could hear Katie pacing in her room. Barbara started to think about Katie and Joshua.

I wonder if anything happened with Katie and Joshua. Things between her and Roy are so uncertain. Is it wise to encourage her to spend time with him? I will take her out tomorrow off the ranch for the day. Joshua can manage without me. Yes, that's what I will do.

Chapter 11

Barbara was up early the following day, excited to be spending some quality time with Katie away from distractions. Katie awoke with a hangover. Her head was killing her, so she threw on her dressing gown and went downstairs to get some painkillers. Joshua was there collecting papers; he smiled as Katie walked past.

“Joshua, you are in charge today me and Katie are going to Houston.” Barbara said.

“Okay Barbara.” Joshua said, as he was leaving.

Katie got some painkillers out of the cabinet and sat down with a glass of water and took the tablets. Then, she buried her head in her hands on the table.

Katie raised her head slowly and looked at Barbara.

“Okay, spill. What have you done? I know that look.” Barbara said.

“What? Nothing, I may have called Roy after I went to bed. I remember him shouting into the phone.”

“Okay but that’s not it. What else did you do last night?”

“Well, I may have possibly sat in your pathway and refused to move, and Joshua may have thrown me over his shoulder.”

“Yeah, that would be it. What were you thinking?”

“That I could do anything I wanted, so why not?”

“Katie, you’re so funny. Do you want pancakes?”

Katie decided to be sensible and call Roy in case she lost track of time again.

“Hello.” said Roy.

“Hi, Roy.”

“Katie have you booked your ticket home yet?”

“No, I haven’t.”

"You need to come home soon. I don't want to talk to you until you see sense!" Roy said.

Roy slammed the phone down.

At least that's done. I am having too much fun to go back home.

Katie was soon ready and was headed downstairs. She really didn't want to think about anything today, she just wanted to have fun with Barbara.

Katie walked downstairs, Barbara was already there,

"Ready to go?"

"Yes, let's go! I haven't been on a shopping day in forever."

"Okay, we're going to a shopping mall, just north of Houston. It's fab."

"Sounds great!"

They drove to the shopping mall and were walking through the parking lot.

I wonder if Joshua is mad at me about last night. Sitting on the floor like that I wouldn't have done it if I hadn't been drunk.

They headed straight to a restaurant for brunch.

"I've never had brunch before." Katie said.

"Why?"

"It's not that big of a thing in England."

"It's great, Katie. You'll love it."

"This is nice, I have missed having a friend so much." Katie said as they sat in the restaurant.

After brunch and they were walking through the mall looking for clothes shops when Barbara asked,

"Have you given any thought to what you're going to do?"

"About what exactly?"

“Well, everything, how long are you going to stay? Will you ever go back to Roy? What is happening between you and Joshua?

“What do you mean? What’s happening between me and Joshua?” Katie asked.

“I noticed you two are quite friendly.”

“He’s easy to get along with. We just talk is all..”

“I would just hate to see him get hurt. He’s like the son I never had.”

“I would never hurt him or anyone..”

“I can stay away from him if you like?”

“I think it’s too late for that. I have seen how he looks at you.”

“Barbara don’t be silly. Anyway, I am not even sure he’s still talking to me after last night..”

Katie walked into a shop and started looking at a red sundress hanging up near the window.

"So, do think you will ever marry again?"

"Stop changing the subject Katie."."

"I'm not. I just wondered."

"Let's go get a Drink."

"Okay, but I'd still like an answer."

Katie nudged Barbara as they walked to a café to get a drink, smiling all the way. Once they had sat down with a drink, Katie asked,

"Are you fed up with me already?"

"Never! You know you are always welcome. But no doubt Roy will want an answer at some point and I just wondered."

"Yes, he is already insisting I go home, I don't want to, his mood doesn't seem to have mellowed in my absence."

"I don't think it will. It's amazing he kept his temper under wraps until now."

"I suppose, I will have to go home eventually. I am just not sure what I want right now."

"Well, at least he can't make you do anything you don't want to."

This would be a great life, just shopping and relaxing with Barbara.

"And no, Katie, I'd never marry again I couldn't imagine loving anyone as much as I loved my husband."

"See that's how it should be. I don't think I have ever loved anyone that way. Well, maybe my horses."

"Maybe you should divorce Roy and marry Goliath instead."

"At least he wouldn't answer back."

"Can we go back and get that red Dress I saw?" Katie asked.

"Okay, course. Let's go."

Katie and Barbara walked back to the dress shop. Katie quickly found the red dress plus several others.

“I think I am going to get this red sundress, what do you think? Katie asked as she held the dress up.

“It’s lovely, but so are the other five. Why not get them all! It’ll give me an excuse to throw lots of parties for you to wear them at” Barbara said.

“You, don’t need an excuse!”

“But it would be better than picking just one.”

“Let’s go to the desk.”

“Katie and Barbara approached the cashier’s desk with the dresses and waited patiently while she packed them. Katie handed the cashier her card.

“Thank you, have a wonderful day” The cashier said.

“You too!” Katie replied.

“I’m feeling really tired now” Katie said to Barbara.

"Let's head home, I'm tired too."

"I can't wait to try my new dress on!"

"Which one? You bought six."

They headed back to the car and went back to the ranch. It wasn't long before they were home having a cup of tea and soaking their feet in bowls. They were surrounded by shopping bags they had just threw anywhere when they got in. Bryan came in.

"Hello Bryan" Barbara and Katie said together.

"Hey" Bryan said.

"What's the matter?"

"Oh, Joshua is in one of his moods, he's being a nightmare. He's down by the river again asked me to drop in this paperwork!"

"Well, what is wrong with him?"

"No idea, but nothing some pie and Katie wouldn't fix."

"Katie?"

"Yes. All I know is Katie disappears for the day and he is all moody."

"Right, I will make the pie, and you can go cheer him up" Barbara said.

"What am I supposed to do?" Katie replied.

"You don't really need to do anything, just be there."

"Bryan, can you show Katie where the river is?"

"Yes, sure."

Katie sat back down. She would refuse, but for some reason Barbara's mind was set. Barbara made an apple pie while Katie and Bryan drank tea.

Barbara knew there was something about the strong connection developing between Katie and Joshua, she just wasn't sure what. And, although her conscience told her she shouldn't be encouraging them to spend time together because Katie was still married to Roy. Barbara wanted Joshua to be happy more. Barbara was thinking about the saying

'Happy worker equals Happy Ranch, and after all I did call it Happy Acres.'

Chapter 12

The apple pie was soon ready, it smelled lovely. Barbara left the pie cooling on the side.

“Well, at least I’ll get some of the pie” Katie said.

“You would think that, wouldn’t you? I have never seen Joshua share pie ever!” Bryan said.

“What? Why?” Katie said.

“I don’t know. It’s a thing he has, he’d give anybody anything but not pie.”

“That’s true Joshua won’t share the pie. I’ll make another one while you are gone. Right off you go you two” Barbara said.

Katie and Bryan left carrying the pie carefully.

“I still don’t understand why I have to give him the pie. How bad a mood is he in exactly?”

"Don't worry; he'll be fine once you give him the pie. Pie solves everything with Joshua doesn't matter what's wrong give him a pie and he's fine. Although he's going to want ice-cream, he's cheeky like that."

"Have you been friends long?"

"I've known him all my life. It's like that around here most of us grew up together."

"It must be nice."

As Katie and Bryan approached the riverbank. Katie could finally see Joshua stood on the riverbank. He had those jeans on again, the ones he was wearing the first time they met.

I wonder if he only has one pair of jeans.

Joshua walked up to Katie.

"What's all this about then?"

Katie pushed the pie into his hands.

"Barbara heard you were upset. She thought the pie would cheer you up."

"Is it apple?"

"Yes, it is."

"So, is there any ice cream?"

"No, sorry."

"Come on." Joshua said.

Joshua started walking in the opposite direction from Bryan and the others. Joshua and Katie found a quiet spot on the riverbank.

"So, are you okay?" Katie asked.

"Yes, I was just feeling a bit off."

"A bit off?"

"Yes, just having a dreadful day I guess."

"Okay. We all feel like that sometimes."

“You’re lucky to have so many people around that care about you.”

“Yes, I am sure you do too. You know back home in the castle.”

“Not really, I barely have friends.”

“Living in a castle must be fun?”

“It’s not as much fun as it sounds.”

“Why not?”

“Well, the prince is boring, and the village is stuck-up.”

“Really?”

“Unfortunately, it’s true. I’d much rather be here.”

“Because watching me eat pie is so interesting.”

“Well, I meant here in Texas.”

“But at least, I get pie when I get back to the house.”

“Is that the highlight of the day?”

"You're so cheeky."

"Thanks."

"So, are you eventually going home to the castle and the prince?"

"I don't know. I suppose I'll have too but right now I just don't want to think about it."

"But you love him, don't you?"

"I thought I did, but now I don't know. I really just want to stay here, but that's hardly practical."

"I hope you get to figure it out."

"Thanks Joshua."

"Come on. Trouble, I'll walk you back to the house."

"Okay, you're not getting my pie though."

As they walked back to the house Katie realized she didn't want to go home ever. She was happy and settled in Texas. This was a surprise to her as it had only been a few days.

As they reached the house, they stopped. Joshua leaned in and gave Katie a hug and said,

“Thank you.”

Katie smiled before walking into the house. When she entered, she saw Barbara standing by the table?

“How did it go?”

“Fine, he was just having a difficult day apparently.”

“Thanks for doing that.”

“You’re welcome. So, any chance of a cup of tea and a slice of pie?”

“Yes. I made you a blueberry pie”

“My favorite. I used to make blueberry jam with my grandmother.”

“Won’t be a minute.”

Katie sat on the sofa. Barbara got some tea and pie and joined her.

"So how was your evening, Barbara?"

"It was very peaceful. Thank you."

After Katie had finished her pie and tea, she went up to bed.

Chapter 13

Katie woke up happy, as she stretched the Texas sunshine burst through the window. She got dressed and went downstairs. Barbara was already at the table working on some paperwork.

"Morning Barbara"

"Morning Katie, there's coffee in the pot"

"Thanks. I was wondering if I could take Goliath out for a ride today?"

"Yes of course. Is Joshua going with you?"

"I hadn't thought about it. Maybe I'll ask him."

Just then Joshua walked in, as he did every morning to check if there was any specific task. Barbara would like him to focus on.

"Ask who what?" Joshua asked.

"I am going to take Goliath out for a ride. Do you want to join me?" Katie asked.

Joshua looked at Barbara.

"Don't look at me. It's nothing to do with me" she said.

"Barbara, it was your idea" Katie said.

"I just asked if he were going with you."

"Yes, I am" said Joshua.

"Katie, just give me a shout when you're ready" Joshua said before leaving again.

"What was that about?" Katie asked.

"Nothing."

They sat there and finished their breakfast in silence. Barbara finished her paperwork and put it in a neat pile in the centre of the table.

"You done" Katie asked.

“Yes, thank you” Barbara said.

Katie cleared the dishes.

“So, are you going to be out all-day Katie?”

“No, probably just an hour or so. I thought I would make you dinner tonight, and we could stay in and spend some time together.”

“Great. That sounds perfect!”

Barbara picked up the paperwork and left. Katie finished her cleaning up and went upstairs to get ready.

Katie started to make her way down towards the stables. Joshua was already there talking to Bryan who was saddling up Goliath.

“You have excellent timing. He’s just about ready” Bryan said.

“Who’s ready, Goliath or Joshua?”

“He means Goliath. I told you I am always ready.”

“Okay. See you later Bryan” Katie said as Bryan walked away.

“Bye Katie. He’s always full of himself too, just so you know.”

“I don’t have to guess who that’s about” Katie said mounting Goliath.

“Hey, come on. Let’s go” Joshua said as he mounted his horse and shook his head in amusement.

“Hey Goliath, we’re going out.”

They all set off.

Joshua started heading down the lane leading off the ranch. Katie was slowly trotting along behind Joshua.

“Am I going to fast?”

“No, I ‘m just following.”

Katie picked up speed until she was side by side with Joshua.

“So where are we going?”

“I thought we would have a trot around Fort Kellna.”

"Great."

Katie dropped back behind Joshua as they turned into the main street. Katie enjoyed seeing all the buildings in the little village town. There were large areas of very green grass with joining paths leading to both the village hall and library. Both were old buildings built in 1829 and had been well kept since. There were a few toddlers playing on the grass, they were looking at the horses. Katie waved as she passed. They were heading out towards the farms on the outskirts of the village. Katie was enjoying the ride.

Joshua is quiet. I hope he's not like this all the time.

"Katie we're going to turn into that farm coming up on the left."

"Okay, are you sure the owners won't mind?"

"I know the owners. It's okay I bring the horses here sometimes."

"Okay. I will follow your lead."

Katie trotted patiently behind Joshua as he led her through the farm, he stopped in the courtyard as a woman approached:

“Morning Joshua! Who’s your friend?”

“Morning Jackie! This is Katie she’s staying at the ranch.”

“Oh, this is Katie? Bryan told me all about her.”

“Hello, Katie! I’m Jackie. How are you enjoying Fort Kellna?” The woman said, moving towards Katie slowly.

“Hello, Jackie! I am enjoying it very well, thank you.”

“Well, you two carry on. I’ll bring you some lemonade in a little while.”

“Bye Jackie!”

“Bye Jackie! Nice to meet you!”

“Jackie is Bryan’s mother. She owns this farm with her husband. Dan.”

“Okay, that’s why you come here then.”

"They are lovely people, and there are always empty fields for the horses to be free in."

Joshua carried on towards the bottom right field and Katie followed him. Most of the farm was quite small, but the right bottom field was bigger. It was fenced in with a gate. The grass wasn't as well kept as on the rest of the farm. Katie and Joshua dismounted, and let the horses roam around the field freely. They went to sit in a corner of the field and watch the horses.

"It's nice here. You do know some nice places" Katie said.

"Yes, I guess just lucky to live in such a lovely place. There are lots to choose from."

"I know I am enjoying myself so much that, I never want to leave."

"Don't you have to at some point? I mean what about the prince. Doesn't he miss you?"

"I think by now, you have probably figured out my relationship and life in Cornwall is not that great."

"I don't want to pry. It was just an observation."

"You're not prying, but if I can find a way to stay in Fort Kellna I will."

"So, you're not just treating this a holiday anymore?"

"It was never a holiday, Joshua. It was an escape."

"An escape from?"

"The man I thought I knew. I don't know why it's so easy to talk to you."

"Maybe you should talk to Barbara about how you are wanting to stay. I am sure she would love to help."

"I will. I am just trying to figure things out. I just always dreamed of a simple life."

"A simple life like what?"

"A little cottage in the middle of nowhere with a barn and, maybe a few horses. Just minding my own business with someone who loves me for me, not their version of me."

"Sounds like a nice little world all of your own" Joshua said as he brushed his hair back.

"So, the castle, the prince, and being rich, is not your dream but his."

"Well, I asked for the castle, so that's kind of my fault. It seemed like a good idea at the time. I don't really care for the money, and the prince isn't who I thought he was. I am not sure I can face him again."

"Then don't. My mother always said if you don't like your life then change it. Yes, it's hard but everything worth having is."

"Your mother sounds very smart."

"She has her moments."

"I really do enjoy these little chats we have Joshua."

“Me to.”

Jackie walked down to the field with a tray with lemonade and glasses. She lay it quietly on the ground, with a note that read:

’Please return the tray to the house on your way out.’

“Yay! Lemonade!” Katie said.

“I’ll pour you some, but seriously, Katie, talk to Barbara.”

“I will. I promise.”

“Here’s your lemonade. “

Katie sat there enjoying her lemonade in the sunshine, watching Goliath in the field.

I wish I could stay forever.

“Let’s head back.”

“Okay, whenever you’re ready, Katie.”

After finishing her lemonade, she jumped to her feet and walked over to Goliath.

"Time to go boy."

Katie took Goliath by the reins and started to walk him out of the field. Joshua got his horse and joined her, collecting the tray of things to return.

"You look like a waiter" Katie said.

"Thanks."

They walked up to the farmhouse. Jackie was just outside.

"Thank you, Joshua" she said, taking the things from him.

"You're welcome. It was delicious!"

"Anytime. Bye Katie."

"Bye, Jackie. Thank you for the lemonade."

Katie and Joshua mounted their horses and began to make their way back to the ranch. They were quiet on the way back: they were just slowly trotting along. Joshua started thinking about Katie.

I know it's wrong. She's married to an idiot but married, nonetheless. I wonder if she knows I can't stop thinking about her, and I have this uncontrollable need to rescue her.

They were almost back at the stables, and Katie was feeling a little sad that they were back.

How can I be married to Roy, but I can't stop thinking about Joshua? I hope he doesn't notice when I am staring at him. I just want to spend every waking moment with him. I can't stop thinking about him. Does that mean I don't love Roy anymore? Let's face it, he would have deserved it. If I have fallen out of love with him after the way he's acted. I don't think I can control my feelings for Joshua. What am I going to do?

Once they were back at the stables. Joshua went to put his horse in its stall and Katie took Goliath to his stall. She hugged Goliath and removed the saddle.

"Oh, Goliath. I think I have gotten myself into another mess. I am good at that."

"Hey, Katie. You all done here."

"Joshua, I didn't see you come in. Yes."

"Good. hope you enjoyed your ride out."

"I did. Thank you for coming with me."

"You're welcome. What are you doing later?"

"Staying in with Barbara. I promised."

"Okay, have fun."

As Katie went to walk past Joshua to leave, he grabbed her arm, gently pulling her in, and kissed her softly. It was perfect. Katie relaxed into his arms while the kiss lingered.

Softly and slowly the kiss ended. Katie felt a little dizzy, but she continued to walk forward and almost into the door.

"Oh my," she said.

"You okay?"

"Yes, I'm fine. I'm going to the house now."

As she left Bryan walked into the stables.

"I saw that." Bryan said.

"Saw what?" Joshua asked.

"You and Katie."

"I have no idea what you are talking about."

Katie continued to the house quickly, swiftly closed the door behind her, and threw herself on the sofa.

Wow oh wow. That was so wrong and so right at the same time. That was the most perfect kiss I have ever had. Now things are complicated. What will Barbara say? She's bound to find out.

Chapter 14

Katie lay there on the sofa for a few minutes, before starting on dinner, she knew exactly what she was going to make. While she was looking for wine, she found Sangria. Once everything was done Katie laid it all out on the table and went to get a shower before Barbara was back. Katie had just returned downstairs when Barbara walked in.

“How was your day?” Katie asked.

“Good. Not as good as yours, so I hear,” Barbara replied with a cheeky smile.

“What do you mean?”

“Well, rumor has it, Joshua kissed you in the stables.”

“Oh, yes... wait how do people know about that?”

“Bryan saw you two.”

“This is going to get complicated. It was our first kiss, and I know it was wrong. I mean, I’m married.”

“Calm down. It’ll be fine, but I do want to hear all about that kiss though.”

“Hold on. Barbara, I just have to take this call.”

Katie answered her phone.

“Hello.”

“Hello Katie, what is going on?”

“Roy, nothing why?”

“I thought you would have come to your senses by now, but I haven’t heard from you.”

“Roy, I have always had my senses. I am enjoying myself and will do so as long as I please.”

“No, I don’t think that’s an option. People are starting to ask questions. You need to come home as soon as possible.”

“No, I really don’t.”

“You are starting to make me look foolish, and I won’t have that Katie.”

"You don't need me for that. You do it quite well yourself."

Roy slammed the phone down, and Katie went back to sit on the sofa.

"Do you want a cup of tea?"

"Oh, yes, please."

"Is everything okay?"

"Yes, just Roy is demanding that I return as soon as possible."

"Are you thinking about that? Going back, I mean."

"To be honest, Barbara, no."

Barbara passed Katie her tea.

"I was going to talk to you tonight because I really don't know what to do," Katie said.

"Let's have dinner, and we can talk, afterward," Barbara said.

"So, what's all this food then?"

"Oh, there's apple wrapped in ham followed by Dutch lemon chicken and salad, followed by madeleines and jam and sangria."

"I didn't know you could cook Dutch food."

"Yes, I learned from the woman I stayed with when I was an exchange student."

"It's really nice. You should teach me."

"Okay. It's really simple."

When they were finished, they made their way over to the sofa with their glasses of Sangria.

"Oh, Katie, bring the bottle with you."

"I will."

"What are you thinking?"

"Well, basically, I don't want to go back to Roy and that life. It was so restrictive. Honestly, I couldn't do anything at all without it being reported back. Everything I did had to be approved by Roy. I don't think I would ever get over him hitting me. It destroyed any feelings I still had for him."

"So, do you want to stay in Texas? Because I would love for you to stay."

"Yes, I would like to stay, too. I am not sure how to go about that, and Roy isn't going to let me go easily. I am a possession to him, nothing else, and I fear what he will do when I tell him. I have some money in my account, but he controls that."

"I can't help you tell Roy, but I do promise you will always be safe here. I have friends that hired help from abroad: you just need a work visa, so you can work with the horses here on the ranch. That's just red tape we can sort it tomorrow and get you your own saving account, so Roy can't take any more money from you. I have to ask, has any of this got anything to do with Joshua?"

"I really like Joshua, but to be honest. I think I knew this would happen before I met him."

"You will need to talk about it with him though, because it changes things, you're no longer a guest."

"I know, I will tomorrow evening. So, do you think this will really work? Do I really get to stay?"

"Of course it will you know there's nothing I can't sort. Now tell me about this kiss!"

"What are you like? Barbara."

"Curious. I am myself what can I say."

"We were in the stables I was leaving and he pulled me in, it was just soft and gentle and amazing. I don't know, there's just something about when I am with Joshua. I mean I can talk to him about anything, and sometimes he's annoying like he must be right all the time. But it's just blissful and I feel like I finally belong somewhere does that make sense?"

"It's make's perfect sense. I just thought it was a bit of fun but sounds like you are pretty smitten!"

"I never really thought about it till now, I guess I am."

"We need wine. Oh, so much wine."

Barbara got up and got a few bottles from the kitchen.

"I am just really happy. I get to stay."

Katie and Barbara drank the night away. One bottle of wine after another until they were both exhausted and headed for bed.

Chapter 15

Katie woke early the following morning. It was a lovely morning. The sun was rising beautifully, birds were singing in the tree outside, and Barbara was playing music downstairs and Joshua had just walked in. Katie performed her usual routine and got showered and dressed for the day. The smell of bacon was so strong that, she hurried downstairs.

"Morning, sleepy head," Barbara said.

"Hey," Katie replied.

"That smells good Barbara," Joshua said.

"Would you like some, Joshua?"

"Yes, please."

"Oh Joshua, Katie and I are going to Houston. I'll be gone most of the day."

"Okay, no problem. I have some paperwork for you to sign but nothing urgent. I will leave it on the table."

"Thank you."

Barbara handed Joshua a bacon sandwich as she brought breakfast to the table, they all eat together, when he was finished Joshua got up to leave.

"Joshua, I'll walk you out," Katie said.

Once they were outside alone, Joshua said,

"I'm sorry about Bryan telling people."

"It's okay. I need to talk to you later. Could we maybe go somewhere private after work?"

"Yes, I will come and get you at the end of the day."

"Great!"

"See you later, Katie."

"Bye, Joshua."

Joshua kissed Katie on the cheek as he left. She turned around, smiled and made her way into the house.

“Let’s go to Houston,” Barbara said.

“Okay, Barbara. Just let me grab my handbag.”

Katie breathed a sigh of relief that she was staying all she had to do was tell Joshua and Roy. He could wait she wasn’t looking forward to telling him and she wanted to enjoy the moment.

Barbara and Katie were soon in Houston. First, they picked up the paperwork for the work visa and then they sorted her bank account. With all her money now safely withdrawn from the old account, Katie was happy. They headed to a café for a drink. Suddenly Katie’s phone rang.

“Katie, why have you withdrawn all your money at once?” Roy asked.

“Hello, to you too, Roy,” Katie said.

"Fine. Hello, now tell me what you're up to?"

"Shopping with Barbara."

"Does that include shopping for a plane ticket home?"

"We'll talk about it later. I am not discussing it in the middle of the street."

"That's a no then."

"Goodbye, Roy."

Katie hung up.

"Do you see what I mean? It took, twenty minutes, and I am not even in Cornwall."

"Drink your latte. You handled it well."

"Thanks."

"So, can I work in the stables? I have always wanted to."

"Yes, that's the plan. I will get you a job description later, but you realize this means working under Joshua's instructions, and you will have to behave."

"He's going to love that. I always behave. I promise to behave during work hours. How's that?"

"I think we can manage that. It's time for some shopping."

Off they went shopping. Katie would need more clothes if she were staying so, she brought jeans, tops, riding clothes, a helmet, and boots. Katie was stood outside the equestrian store.

I get to go horse riding anytime I want this is going to be great.

Katie and Barbara finished their shopping. Katie felt happier than she had for a long time. She was having a great day with Barbara. Barbara was overjoyed that Katie was staying; she couldn't bear the thought of Katie returning to Roy after what he had done. It would have broken her heart. Barbara was thinking about another party, Katie could take or leave them, but Barbara loved parties. Barbara was planning about the party in her head.

A party at the end of the week to celebrate Katie staying. Fewer people this time, I think I'll keep the invites to thirty, so she doesn't get overwhelmed. She thinks I didn't notice last time, that she struggled to cope with the crowd, but I did.

Chapter Sixteen

Katie and Barbara were sitting down in the house, exhausted from their shopping trip. Surrounded by shopping bags just left anywhere there was a space.

"Don't you have plans to see Joshua soon?"

"Oh, yes I'd forgotten all about that."

"He finishes work in about 45 minutes. You might want to get ready."

"Yes, I guess, just two more minutes to relax."

Katie sat there for two more minutes, before reluctantly getting to her feet. She took a few bags and headed upstairs. She reappeared a little time later dressed in a little blue top, jeans and sandals. her hair was down.

"Do I look okay?"

"You look really lovely."

"Thank you. I haven't a clue how I am going to tell him about me staying?"

"Just be honest, and you'll be fine."

"I suppose."

"Are you nervous?"

"A little. I am not sure what he will think."

"Joshua is a nice guy. I am sure it will go just fine."

"Evening, Barbara. Did you get around to that paperwork I left you?"

"Hi, Joshua. Not yet I will have a look at it tonight."

"Okay, great."

"Hi Joshua."

"Hi Katie, you look nice, ready to go?"

"Yes."

"Have a nice evening, Barbara," Katie said, as she took Joshua's hand.

"Since you said you wanted to talk. I thought we would go down by the riverside. There's a secret den!"

"A den? How old are you exactly?"

Joshua laughed "It's very grown up, I assure you."

"Okay, I am just glad I didn't wear a dress."

"There was me thinking you had a sense of adventure!"

"Says the boy who never left Fort Kellna."

Joshua led Katie to the riverside and there was a little bank with some trees and a clearing in sight. They headed towards the clearing: inside the clearing was a small den. There were three seats made from tree stumps and a large branch that covered the entrance like a door. The sunshine lit the whole space up nicely. They went inside and sat down.

"Okay, so who comes here?"

"Usually me, Bryan and our friend Gerry."

"Okay. It seems like a nice place to escape to."

"So, are you going to tell me what this is all about?"

"I have some news, and I am not sure, how you are going to take it."

"It can't be that bad," Joshua said, his mind started to race thinking.

I hope she's not going home already.

"I'm just going to say it before I lose my nerve too."

"Please do."

"I talked to Barbara last night, and we came up with a plan for me to stay here for good. Well eventually I would need to get a place of my own, but you get the idea."

Katie nervously watched Joshua's face for an expression. A smile slowly spread across his face, and then he closed his lips, to hide it. As Katie watched him, she was thinking.

God, I love that smile.

“So, you’re never going back to Cornwall, the castle and the prince?”

“There’s a lot you don’t knowJoshua but no, I could never go back to him now. I want to stay here forever.”

“That’s an intriguing development. So, you’re going to live with Barbara for a while?”

“Yes, I am going to work in the stables too. We are doing the paperwork, so it’s all legal.”

“You mean, you are coming to work with me?”

“Yes, I’m hoping that’s not a problem.”

“Oh, no not at all. I am looking forward to you doing as you’re told for once.”

“Hey, I am not that bad. Am I?”

“Sometimes.”

“It will be great. I am glad you decided to stay.”

"Thank you. I am really happy."

"You're welcome."

Joshua leaned forward, gently put his hands on Katie's face and kissed her slowly. Katie leaned in and kissed him back. She always felt safe with Joshua, and when he put his arms around her, she got this warm happy feeling inside her soul. She had heard people talk about feeling like that but never experienced it herself. Joshua suddenly stopped and leaned back.

"Have you told him?" he asked.

"Oh my, you know how to ruin a moment, don't you?"

"Sorry, but it's important, Katie. Have you told him?"

"No, not yet"

"You need to, the sooner, the better."

"I know. I am going to do it tomorrow. I am a bit scared, to be honest, he has the worst temper."

"He can't hurt you here, Katie. I wouldn't let him."

"Like I said there's a lot you don't know."

"You can fill me in some other time," Joshua said putting his arm around Katie and turning his head.

"Look over there above the grass."

"Wow, fireflies."

"Yes, let's go and sit on the riverbank."

"Okay."

They went out of the clearing and sat on the riverbank, watching the moon's reflection in the river. Joshua was walking Katie back to the house. He kissed her goodbye outside the door and left. Katie watched him disappear.

She entered the house slowly with a smile on her face and her arms gently folded.

"Good evening, Katie."

"Hi, Barbara. How was your night?"

"Oh, it was okay. You know, just doing paperwork."

"How did it go?"

"Yes, it went okay. He told me I need to tell Roy soon," Katie said.

"Well, he's right about that."

"I know, I sometimes wonder what I did before Joshua's wise counsel."

The two of them burst into laughter.

"You're so dramatic sometimes. Want some tea?"

"Yes, please. So that's done. I will tell Roy tomorrow."

"That's my girl. It will soon be all sorted and we can get back to normal. Oh, I did the paperwork while you were out. You need to sign in a couple of places I put tabs on for you."

"Okay, can I do it tomorrow? I am so tired. I just want a cup of tea and then bed."

"Of course, whenever you're ready."

Chapter 17

The following day Katie got up early, Barbara was sat at the table. She was having a working breakfast, Katie made a pot of tea and went over to join her. Katie sat and signed all the paperwork formalizing her job offer as a stable hand and finished the application for the work visa.

“Morning Barbara, would you like some tea?”

“Thanks Katie. You’re a star.”

“I am going to phone Roy later, but I thought I would take Goliath out on a ride if that’s okay.”

“Sure. Maybe it will help you work out what to tell Roy.”

“Maybe it will, I hope so.”

“I have some work to do so I will be in and out all day, but I will be around.”

“Great!”

Katie was riding Goliath; it was lovely and peaceful. The sun was shining in a clear sky, and Goliath was in excellent form, as always.

“I love to go out riding with you, boy,” Katie said to Goliath.

“And now we can go out more because I am never going to leave you again.”

“I love you.”

Sometimes I think I love Goliath more than any person I know. We have such a special bond; he doesn’t argue with me, and I can be myself without the fear of judgment. It’s such a magical thing.

There was a clearing in the woods. Katie stopped a while to rest, the clearing led down to a stream. Katie took Goliath to the stream to drink as it was such a hot day. While he was drinking, Katie took off her boots and socks and dipped her feet in the stream, it was lovely and refreshing. There was something about wearing no shoes that made Katie free and wild. Katie and Goliath stayed by the stream a while. It was soon time to go back to the ranch and face calling Roy to tell him she was never coming back. Katie was not looking forward to it, she was never sure how he would respond. After all these things rarely play out how she imagined. Katie took a deep breath, got back on Goliath and slowly rode back to the ranch.

Katie made her way into her bedroom and shut the door. She sat on the bed, took a deep breath, and dialed Roy's number.

Here we go.

"Hello," Roy said.

"Hello, Roy."

"Katie, have you finally come to your senses?"

"Yes, but not in the way you think."

"What exactly does that mean? You either booked a ticket to come home or you didn't."

"I did not, but I have come to a decision."

"I am listening."

"I can't come home because my home is here."

"What?"

"I am never coming home. I am staying Texas for good."

"Don't be crazy, Katie. You can't stay in Texas. You're English for a start."

"I found a way. I am staying here. I can't forgive you for what you did. I don't want to see you again."

"Is there someone else? You know you can't get married there. I will never let you go."

"No, this is about the kind of life I want. You need to let me go. I'm sorry."

"I don't believe you. I think you are just trying to hurt me. Must be your hormones or something."

"I am very serious. I can't come back ever."

“No, I refuse to believe that. I know you love me and you will come back when the novelty of Texas wears off. I will wait.”

“Roy, please you need to believe me. I don’t want you to wait for something that’s never going to happen.”

“It will happen, Katie. You will see. You don’t mean any of this. You'll come home before the month is out.”

“I’m sorry, I won’t. But I can tell you are not going to listen to me, so I am going now.”

“Katie!”

“Bye, Roy.”

Katie was not sure that the phone call had achieved anything, but at least she had done it. She headed back downstairs, where Barbara was waiting.

“How did it go?”

“He does not believe I mean it, and he thinks I will be home before the month is out.”

"Oh, my. He's a piece of work."

"Yes, he is. At least I did it, and hopefully time will show him I'm serious."

"Come on. I'm proud of you. Let's have a whiskey."

"I could use one."

Barbara filled two glasses, handed one to Katie, and said,

"To the future. May it happy."

"To the future"

Katie threw the whiskey down her throat and it burned a little as it went down.

To my new life.

Chapter 18

The following day, Katie was up early and excited. Today was her first day working in the stables. She got up washed, dressed and headed downstairs. When she hit the bottom of the stairs, Barbara said.

“It's been a long time since I have seen you dressed that way.”

Katie was wearing blue jeans, a coral vest, riding boots and her hair was tied back neatly in a ponytail.

“Do I look okay?”

“Yes, you look fine.”

“I am so excited.”

“Come have some breakfast.”

Katie had some tea and toast.

“Do you have any plans today?” Katie said.

"I am going to file your paperwork this morning and, then just do a few jobs in town."

"Okay, great."

"Morning, Katie! Morning, Barbara!" said Joshua as he walked in.

"Morning, Joshua," they both replied.

"Katie, you ready for work?"

"Yes, pretty much."

"I'll walk you down to the stables then."

"Bye, Barbara."

"Bye, Katie. Be sure to have fun."

Katie and Joshua left, closing the door behind them.

"So how are things with you?" Joshua said.

"I am really excited about working in the stables."

"That will wear off, I expect. You will be working with Bryan today. He will show you where everything is and what to do and when."

"Great! He seems nice."

"Yeah, he is."

"So, what did you do yesterday?" Joshua asked.

"I went for a ride on Goliath and talked to Roy."

"Did you tell Roy?"

"I did, but he doesn't believe me."

"At least you told him."

"Yes, I am glad I got it over with."

"Good. Well, good luck today. I will see you a bit later."

"Thank you."

As Joshua left, Katie walked into the stables and Bryan walked towards Katie.

"Hello, Katie."

"Hello, Bryan."

"So, we work in teams. Today you're with me and Alex."

A man with very deep brown hair and hazel brown eyes, who was tall wearing a T-shirt and jeans approached Katie.

"Hiya, Katie I'm Alex."

"Hello, Alex."

"Yeah, we are taking the horses to the field first while the other team, Justin, Janet and Theo muck out the stables, so let's go," Bryan said.

They each got two horses each and walked them down to the bottom field. Katie followed Bryan, so she didn't make a mistake, and Alex walked to the side, occasionally smiling at her. Katie was unsure why, but she just carried on. He seemed pleasant enough, but his staring was making her feel a bit uncomfortable. Katie was relieved when they got to the field. Bryan locked the gate and they let the horses roam free. Goliath stayed by Katie's side. Katie thought he could probably sense she was feeling uncomfortable, her horses were good at that sort of thing.

"So, Katie. You and Joshua. What's the deal with that?" Alex asked.

"Oh, Lord. Here we go," Bryan whispered.

"Excuse me?" Katie said.

"I heard you two were sort of a thing and, then I heard you were married. So, which is it?"

"Alex, really, are you going to do this now?"

"Yeah, I am."

"It's okay, Bryan. Basically, Alex, is it? It's none of your business and maybe if you concentrated on your own life, you wouldn't be so interested in mine."

"Oh, okay, fair enough."

Bryan laughed.

"He hasn't been told off like that since the second grade."

Katie blushed and then laughed out loud. Alex was quiet after that, and Bryan was thankful he was. Katie enjoyed watching the horses in the field. Her first day's work was going well. In the afternoon, the teams switched, and Katie got to muck out the stables. Although it was dirty, smelly, and challenging work she enjoyed it. At least she didn't have to make conversation. At the end of the day. Joshua came to see how she was getting on.

Once Katie was back at the house, sitting on the sofa with Barbara she asked.

"So, what's for dinner I am so hungry!"

"Anything you want. Just tell me what you fancy."

"Oh, Chinese. I want pork balls with Peking sauce."

"Okay, let me see if Joshua wants to join us and then he can get it."

Barbara disappeared into the kitchen to call Joshua. Katie snuggled into the sofa with a smile.

"That's sorted then. Joshua is going to pick up the food and join us for tea."

"Yay! I love Chinese food!"

"We have to celebrate your first day working."

"True. We have wine, too."

Barbara sat on the sofa with Katie, watching television, until Joshua appeared with a bag of food. Barbara jumped up. It, wasn't long before they were all sat around the table, with wine and food, enjoying themselves, Barbara raised a toast:

"To Katie on her first day of work. Well done, Katie!"

"Well done, Katie!"

"Thank you, both."

"Bryan said you did really well," Joshua said.

"Did he? Great! I really enjoyed it."

After they finished dinner, Joshua said,

"Thank you, Barbara, for inviting me tonight."

"You're welcome. Joshua, anytime."

"Katie, would you mind if we went for a walk?"

"That would be lovely, Joshua."

"Great. Anytime you're ready."

Katie glanced at Barbara.

"Don't mind me."

"Thank you."

"Joshua, let's go."

Joshua and Katie left and walked down towards the river.

"So how are you feeling after your first day?"

“Good. A bit achy but good.”

“Great. I heard about Alex.”

“Alex?”

“Questioning you about me. I heard you handled him well. Bryan told me.”

“Oh that. Well, yes, I guess. Bryan certainly got a giggle out of it.”

“Yes, I bet.”

“You know, more people might ask questions like that.”

“Yes, I was being serious when I told him it’s no-one’s business. The thing is, I am just starting to figure things out for myself. I am not about to start talking to strangers about things I don’t understand myself.”

“That’s a good point.”

“I just wanted you to be aware.”

“Thank you. It's sweet of you.”

"So, do you know what you are going to next?"

"Well, I am thinking of doing a horse care course at the local college."

"That sounds like a good idea."

"Yes, I thought I would ask Barbara to take me to inquire tomorrow afternoon."

"Good luck! I hope it goes well."

"Thank you, Joshua. Are you okay?"

"I think so. I think I just wanted to spend some time with you, without, everyone talking about it. I don't really like people talking about me. It always makes me feel as if I have done something wrong."

"Aww bless you. There's a sensitive soul in there after all."

"Thanks, Katie."

"I do agree though. But unless we get off the ranch, there's not much chance of that."

“So how about tomorrow I take you on a date off the ranch? Somewhere we can just relax.”

“I’d love that. Do we have to call it a date though?”

“What would you call it?”

“Just hanging out together.”

“Okay, Tomorrow, we will just hang out somewhere in town.”

“That sounds great.”

“I better get back, before Barbara sends a search party.”

“Yeah, it’s time I was headed home, too.”

Joshua walked Katie back up to the house and said goodnight, and then left. Katie was feeling tired now. So, she said goodnight to Barbara too and headed off to bed.

Chapter 19

Katie had work the following day, but just for a few hours in the morning. She was up early as usual and made her way downstairs. Barbara was munching fruit in the kitchen while reading some forms.

“Morning, Barbara.”

“Morning Katie.”

“Can we have a little chat?”

“Yeah, sure. What’s the matter?”

“I was thinking I would like to enroll in a horse care course at the local college. Could you take me there this afternoon to go talk to someone?”

“Of course! I think it’s a grand idea. We’ll leave just after lunch.”

“Great! Better get off to work now.”

Katie took a banana to eat on her way down to the stables. Work that day was pretty much the same as the day before. Alex was friendly, but he didn't ask any more awkward questions, and Bryan was delightfully chatty as always. The morning went by fast, and Katie was glad she was excited to go to the college and see what they had to offer. Katie was excited to get to spend time with Joshua, but she couldn't help thinking she should feel guilty because she was still married. In the end, none of it mattered. She couldn't stay away from Joshua if she tried. Why, should she? The marriage was over now anyway, even if Roy did refuse to believe it.

At lunchtime, Katie made her way up to the house. Barbara had made lunch.

"There you are. I hope you're hungry."

"A little. It looks lovely."

"Yeah. It's just something I threw together while you were working."

They sat down at the table and started eating. It was nice to just relax with Barbara.

"So, college. Are you sure you are ready for that?"

"Yes, I am actually really excited about it."

"Okay. We will drive down after lunch and see what we can sort out."

Katie and Barbara headed straight to the local college. They had the exact course Katie wanted so she signed up then and there.

"Well, that was easy enough." Katie said.

"Are you all done?"

"Yes, all signed up and everything."

"Great, let's go shopping."

Katie and Barbara headed into Houston, to go shopping. It was not long before they were in the mall. While they were browsing around the shops. Katie spotted the perfect rucksack for college. It was turquoise and white, it had lots of room and little pockets.

"Oh Barbara, look at this! Isn't it perfect?"

"Yes, that's very you. you should get that."

"Yes, I am going to."

They continued shopping and a little while later, Barbara found a lilac dress. It was long and had sequins down the sides.

"I am going to get this. It's lovely."

"It is. Is it for anything special?"

"Well, I was thinking we could have a small party to celebrate you staying."

"We just had a party."

"Yeah, I know. It won't be a big one like that. Just twenty people or so."

"Okay. How about only twenty peopleand we have an outdoor tea party instead?"

"That sounds perfect."

"Oh, can we invite Cordy? I liked her."

"Yes, sure we will invite John and the family, so no one feels left out."

"Great! Now I need a dress."

"Katie, you have lots of dresses."

"Yes, but I love buying new ones."

"Okay. Let's find you a dress."

"Oh, I forgot to tell you. I am going out with Joshua tonight. We are going into town somewhere."

"Like a date?"

"I really do hate that word. It puts so much pressure on us. We just want to spend time together without the whole ranch talking about it."

"Sounds fun. I bet he takes you bowling. Joshua loves bowling, and he's supposed to be pretty good."

"Really? I like bowling too, but it's been a while."

"Oh wow, Barbara, look! That dress is amazing."

Katie was pointing towards a dressing hanging up in the shop window. It was white cotton and very long. It was a halter neck dress with a low back and a pink ribbon around the waist with thousands of diamante crystals on the ribbon.

"That is something else." said Barbara.

"This is the dress I am getting."

"For the party?"

"Yes. Why?"

"Nothing, it's stunning."

Barbara couldn't argue. It was stunning, but it was a little sexier than she would have chosen, but then Katie had her own style and a strong mind. Barbara knew better than to try and talk her out of something she had set her mind to. Katie went to the shop and bought the dress. She came out of the shop with a big smile on her face.

"Ready to go?" Barbara asked.

They returned to the ranch.

Later, Katie was lying on the bed, must have layed there for about an hour before she finally got ready to go out. She slowly walked downstairs because she didn't want to wake Barbara up who was fast asleep on the sofa. Katie quietly sat at the dining table and began reading her course information. She hadn't been sat there long when Joshua walked in.

"Hello, Katie."

"Hi, Joshua. Shhh... Barbara is asleep," Katie whispered.

"Okay, are you ready to go?"

"Yes, I am ready."

They both quietly left and shut the front door behind them.

Chapter 20

“You look nice tonight.” Joshua said.

“Thank you. So, where are we going?” Katie asked.

“I thought bowling.”

“Great.”

“Oh, good. So, you do like bowling.”

“I love it, but it’s been a while since I have been, so I probably won’t be any good.”

“I am sure you will do just fine, Katie.”

They got into Joshua’s car and drove into town. In no time at all, they were parking outside the bowling alley.

As they walked in Joshua went to the desk. Katie stood behind him. Joshua appeared to know the assistant. He got their bowling shoes and paid. Katie kept following Joshua until he stopped at a bowling lane, and they sat down to put their bowling shoes on. The bowling balls were so shiny sitting on the rack. It seemed like they were waiting to be picked up. Katie was hoping she could use the neon pink one. Joshua was programming the scoring computer with their names while Katie sat and watched him.

"Want to go first?" Joshua asked.

"Okay, then."

Katie walked over to the ball rack. The neon pink ball was just perfect for her. She walked towards the lane, threw the bowling ball, turned around and walked back. She didn't look to see where the ball went. It was a strike.

"Yay!" Katie said.

"Probably won't be any good you said."

"Just lucky I guess."

Joshua laughed. "Maybe."

Joshua stood up to bowl. He threw the ball and then stood there to see where it would go. It was a strike too.

"Well done," Katie said.

"Thanks."

They continued to bowl. Katie was ever so slightly ahead on the scoreboard. About three-quarters of the way through the game,Joshua's friend Leo, who worked at the bowling alley came over with a tray of drinks.

"Hey, Joshua. I thought you could use a drink," Leo said.

"Thanks, Leo. Katie this is my friend, Leo."

"Hello, Leo. Thanks for the drink."

Leo looked at the scoreboard and said,

"Wow, Joshua getting beaten by a girl."

"My name is Katie," she said.

"Okay, sorry, Katie."

Joshua laughed. "See you later Leo," Joshua said, as Leo walked away.

"Bye, Katie."

"Bye, Leo."

They continued to bowl, and Katie won the game. They sat down to wait for the bowling lane to reset.

"Well done. You're really good," Joshua said.

"Thanks. You are, too."

"One last game then."

"Yes, that sounds good."

Katie and Joshua continued to bowl for one last game and Katie won. If it were anyone

else Joshua's pride would have been bruised, but he'd let Katie get away with almost anything. They decided to leave.

"Bye, Leo," they both said as they passed him on the way out.

"Bye, Joshua! Bye, Katie!" he replied.

They made their way back to Joshua's car. Katie was standing by the passenger door. Joshua put his hand on the roof of the car and leaned in, resting his other hand on Katie's waist. He gently kissed her. It was a soft, lingering kiss. Joshua said.

"It's nice kissing you when no-one is around."

"I just like it when you kiss me," Katie said.

They both got into the car.

"I thought we could go sit by the river for a while," Joshua said.

"That would be nice."

Joshua drove them to the river, and they walked down and sat on the riverbank. It was very calm and quiet. The dark sun had started to fall, and the stars were starting to appear. The moonlight was shimmering on the water. Joshua put his arm around Katie, and she smiled at him.

"This is lovely, Joshua."

"Yes, it is."

"You're a very private person, aren't you?"

"I try to be Katie. It's hard in this small town, especially as Bryan is my best friend."

Katie laughed "Yes, he does love to gossip."

Katie shook her hair back and looked at Joshua.

"Oh, by the way, I registered for college."

"Great. Is that to do horse care?"

"Yes, I am really excited."

"I think you are going to love it and it will be good for you to meet some new people."

"Yes, it always makes me nervous at first, but it's good to have friends."

"Seems, like you're settling in well."

“I hadn’t thought of it, but I guess I am.”

Katie cuddled into Joshua, to watch the river and the moonlight. It was almost as if it were dancing on top of the river now. Katie didn’t really want to talk, she just wanted to sit there, so they did. Joshua was happy just to be close to her and not have to worry about anyone judging. There were a lot of stars in the night sky. They were glittering like a thousand crystals scattered on a backdrop. It started getting late.

“Come on. Katie. I will drive you up to the house.”

“Thank you. I have had a great night. Joshua.”

“Good. I’m glad.”

They got into the car and Joshua drove Katie to the house. When the car stopped Katie slowly leaned in and kissed him goodnight before getting out the car.

“Good night, Joshua.”

"Good night, Katie."

Katie slowly walked towards the door, and Joshua watched until she was safely inside and then drove away. Barbara was up waiting for Katie. She was making hot chocolate in the kitchen.

Chapter 21

The following day. Joshua decided to take Katie out to dinner that evening. He asked her at lunchtime, and she had agreed. Joshua walked into the house, Barbara was in the kitchen making coffee and Katie had just come downstairs.

"Good evening, Katie. Are you ready?" Joshua asked.

"Yes, I am ready to go."

"Going out again twice in one week. Must be serious," Barbara teased.

"Ha-ha. Stop being nosy," Katie said.

They quickly left and drove away.

"So, where are we going tonight?" Katie asked.

"There's this great restaurant. It does steak any way you want it and has the best milkshakes in town. I thought we could try it."

"Sounds, great! Two of my favorite things."

"Great!"

They soon arrived at the restaurant. It didn't look much from outside, but inside was very pretty. There were little round tables with pink and white tablecloths and a single pink rose in a white vase on each table. There were some bigger tables on a platform, a few steps up on the far side of the restaurant and a milkshake bar where you could get a milkshake made from any of the various ice creams on display. They sat down at one of the little tables. There was soft classical music playing in the background.

"So, do come here a lot?" Katie asked, glancing at the menu.

"Not really. I have been here maybe twice before."

The waitress appeared and said,

"Are you ready to order? Can I get you a drink while you decide?"

Joshua looked at Katie.

"Do you know what you want?"

"Yes. Can I have a strawberry milkshake and a well-done steak? When I say well done, I mean almost burnt."

"I will have a banana milkshake and a medium rare steak. Thank you."

Katie had no idea what a medium rare steak looked like because she had never eaten with anyone who eats steak that way.

"I like a girl who can make up her mind quickly," Joshua said.

"Thank you."

"How was your day today, Katie?"

"It was good, thanks. Was your day okay?"

"Yes, it was good."

The food arrived, and Katie started sipping her milkshake. The food looked so good. Katie watched Joshua as he took a sip of his milkshake and took the steak knife. Katie could see blood oozing out of the steak as he cut into it. She thought she was going to be sick. She suddenly realized what medium rare meant. She couldn't eat while that steak was on his plate, so she tried to look anywhere but at Joshua and that steak. In between mouthfuls, Joshua asked:

"Are you all right, you're not eating?"

"Yes, kind of, I can't stand the sight of blood, I'll eat in a minute"

"Oh, you should have said earlier. I 'm sorry."

"It's okay, I will be okay in a minute."

Joshua soon finished his steak. He cleaned his plate with a napkin to remove any excess blood. So, Katie would feel more comfortable. Katie sipped her milkshake and cautiously cut into her steak. It was perfectly done so she need not have worried. When she finished Katie said,

"That was really nice. Thank you for bringing me here."

"You're welcome. I am glad you liked it."

"It's nice to have spent time with you."

"I like spending time with you, too, Katie."

"I'm glad."

"Ready to go?"

"Yes, I am."

Joshua paid the bill, and they left. Katie held Joshua's hand as they walked across the parking lot to his car.

As they got into the car Joshua kissed Katie. It was slow and passionate. He gently held her face as he kissed her. Katie didn't want it to end, but when it did end, she asked.

"Joshua, can we go talk?"

"Yes, sure! Is everything ok?"

"Yes, I just want to talk. That's all."

"We can talk here." he said.

"Thank you."

"So, Katie, what's on your mind?"

"Me and you? I mean what's actually going on here?"

"That's quite a huge question, Katie. It's hard to know where to start."

"Okay, I can't believe I'm saying this, but I going to. I am never going back to Roy, but I am still technically married. I know people are talking, and I don't want to have to justify this. But Joshua, if there is anything between us, I want to be free to explore that and spend time with you."

"Wow. That's a lot. For a start. I am glad you're not going back. You should know what it's like around here by now. This is Fort Kellna. If they weren't talking about us, it would just be something else they were talking about, it's gossiping, it is what people in this town do. But you don't have to justify anything to anyone because it is no-one else's business really. I don't know what is between us, but I know I want to spend time with you. I'm happy when we spend time together. But if there's something you feel you need to do, just do it."

"Spending time with you, makes me happy, too. I just wanted to be sure you were prepared for the gossip that's bound to start. I haven't figured out how to convince Roy I am never coming back, to be honest. I am just enjoying being here."

Joshua leaned, gave Katie a hug and said,

"You have all the time in the world to figure this out. Don't worry people don't really care what we do. It is just because it's something new to talk about."

"I hope you're right," Katie replied.

"Come on, let's get you back."

"Okay, I have college tomorrow."

"Oh, yeah. Good luck with that."

Joshua drove Katie back to the house. He stopped, turned the engine off and leaned over and kissed her softly.

“Goodnight, Katie.”

“Goodnight, Joshua, and thank you for dinner.”

“You're very welcome.”

Chapter 22

The following morning, Barbara and Katie left for the college. Barbara drove them in her car. It didn't take very long.

"Well. Here we are, good luck," Barbara said

"Thank you, I will see you later I finish at 4 p.m.," Katie said.

Katie got out of the car and looked at the building in front of her. She put her bag on her shoulder. The building was made of sandy stone with large glass windows and two floors. It had steps that led up to the door. Katie slowly made her way towards the entrance and took a deep breath.

Katie stepped inside and up to the reception desk. The woman behind the desk looked very tidy and smart dressed in a white blouse and navy-blue blazer with brown hair tied back perfectly and hazel eyes and a kind smile.

"Welcome to Fort Kellna College. Can I help you?" she said.

"Yes, I am looking for the Horse Care level 1 class. I am new" Katie said.

"Katelyn! Come here. Will you show? Sorry I didn't catch your name?" she asked.

"It's Katie"

Katelyn approached Katie. She looked to be about twenty-two years old. She had long blond wavy hair and blue eyes. She had a slim build. Katelyn had a cream blouse and white jeans on with a blue cardigan draped across her arm.

"Can you show Katie to class please Katelyn?" the woman said.

"Yes. Of course," Katelyn said.

Katie politely followed Katelyn to the classroom.

"So, are you new in town?" Katelyn asked

"Yes, sort of I am staying with my friend Barbara- at Happy Acres Ranch."

“Oh, yes, everyone knows Barbara.”

“Yeah, so I am learning!”

“Well, this is our room. Don’t worry, you will soon find your way around. If you need any help, just ask.”

“Thank you. Katelyn.”

Katie really enjoyed her first day at college. They studied the nutrition module of the course, and she found it very interesting. There was a lot of information to take in. The day flew by. Katie ate her packed lunch on the grass with Katelyn and a few other girls from the class. They only got 45 minutes for lunch. Katie was happy but was looking forward to going home and relaxing on the sofa. She was tired even though she had sat all day. It was soon time to go home. When Katie walked out of the building Barbara was waiting for her.

“Bye, Katelyn,” Katie said, as she walked out of the building and towards Barbara’s car.

“Bye, Katie! See you next week,” Katelyn said.

“Hi, Barbara!” Katie said, getting into the car.

“Hi, Katie! How was your day?” Barbara asked.

“It was good, thanks. How was your day?”

“It was okay, let’s go home.”

They were soon back at the ranch, and Katie sat on the sofa with a cup of tea.

“I see you met Katelyn today, she’s a sweet girl,” Barbara said

“Yes, she showed me around. She seemed nice.”

“You look tired. Was its hard work?”

“No, it was great, but there’s a lot to take in and I have homework but, I will do it tomorrow when I am not so tired”

“Okay, so what do you what for dinner?”

“Can we just get pizza and have a glass of wine and relax on the sofa? I really just want to do as little as possible tonight.”

"Okay, Katie. I will find you a menu. You can choose a pizza."

"Great"

Katie sat on the sofa drinking her tea while Barbara went to the kitchen to look for a menu.

"Hi Katie, Hi Barbara," Joshua said as he came in.

"All done for the day," Joshua said.

"Okay, see you tomorrow," Barbara said.

"Here's the menu. Katie!" Barbara said.

"Thanks."

"I think. I will just get a veggie feast pizza," Katie said.

"Great! I will order it now," Barbara said.

"Okay, it's so nice to relax"

"I think you need an early night"

"Probably, it's because I am not used to it."

"I think it's really good how well you've settled in. You are working in the stables and now going to college."

"I do feel happy, I think it's all very good for me."

"And we have your party on Saturday."

"Oh, I had almost forgotten about that!"

"It will be fun, and a nice end to a good week."

"I kept the numbers down to twenty-five people, so it won't be too crowded."

"Thank you."

The pizza soon arrived, and Barbara opened a bottle of wine. Katie sat on the sofa with the TV playing in the background while she ate dinner and drank the wine. Katie was so tired that she went to bed straight after dinner, she fell asleep instantly. She woke early the following day feeling very refreshed. Katie worked in the stables until lunch, and then she went shopping with Barbara for a new dress for the party, which was the following day.

Katie brought along pink maxi dress and some sandals. Katie spent the evening with Joshua. They just sat by the river and talked just as they had done before. She enjoyed talking to Joshua and valued his advice.

The following morning Barbara revealed the details of Katie's party. Barbara had kept a calmer, simpler plan this time. There would be a three-course meal served in a tent. All the guests would be around a table. There would be caterers and waitresses as well as lots of wine and soft music. Katie was so happy, it sounded perfect. She was excited. Barbara had invited Cordy, Lynette, and Katelyn. Katie and Barbara spent most of the day getting ready for the party. Joshua and the staff of the ranch took care of the arrangements and made sure everything was ready for the evening.

It was 7 p.m., and it was finally time for the party. Katie and Barbara were both ready. They headed down to the bottom field. Barbara held all her parties in the bottom field. Katie walked into the tent Joshua pulled her chair out for her.

"Thank you, Joshua," Katie said.

Barbara sat at the head of the long banquet table.

"Thank you, everyone, for coming, we are here to celebrate the fact that Katie has decided to stay in Fort Kellna."

Everyone clapped loudly, Katie smiled.

"Thank you," Katie said.

Everything looked so pretty. The banquet table was covered with a white tablecloth. There were pink metallic hearts scattered all over the table. There were also pink candles and pink floating flowers in little bowls. There was also a pink floral centerpiece. The chairs were covered in white satin. There were groups of white and pink balloons in each corner of the tent. The waitresses started to serve the appetizers. They were popcorn shrimp and salad, Katie's favorite.

"Thank you. Barbara. This is great; I love it," Katie said.

"You are more than welcome."

Katie really enjoyed her dinner party. She was very happy. Barbara had included all her favorite foods, and everyone seemed to be enjoying themselves. The conversation flowed all evening. Katie drank probably a bit too much wine. But it was all perfect. At the end of the evening, Katie thanked everyone for coming. One by one they all left, and Barbara had disappeared to talk to some people. Only Katie and Joshua were left in the tent.

"Joshua, dance with me," Katie said.

"Here and now? Are you sure?"

"Yes, I am sure! I want to dance!"

"Okay, then."

Joshua walked up to Katie, put his arms around her, and danced slowly. Katie put her head on his shoulder as they danced around in circles.

"Tonight, was so perfect," Katie said.

"Barbara, will be happy when you tell her that."

"I know! I am so glad I stayed."

"I am, too."

Joshua leaned in and kissed Katie slowly. When he was finished, he said,

"Come on, let's get you back to the house."

"Okay. I am getting tired."

Katie took Joshua's hand, and they slowly made their way back up towards the house. Joshua waited for Katie to go inside, before leaving to go home himself. When Katie got inside, Barbara was on the sofa.

"Hello, Barbara! This is where you went."

"Hello, Katie! Yes, I am tired."

"Thank you for the party. It was perfect."

"I am glad you enjoyed it. Katie."

"I did. I am off to bed, Barbara. I think all that wine went to my head."

"Good night, Katie."

"Good night, Barbara."

The following morning, Katie woke up late. She was glad it was Sunday. She got ready and headed downstairs. Barbara must have slept in too because she was just making breakfast.

"Breakfast will be ready in a minute, help yourself to orange juice," Barbara said.

"Thanks. Can we have a chat about something over breakfast?" Katie asked.

"Sure, I am all yours all day!"

"Great!"

Katie sat down at the dining table and poured herself a glass of orange juice. It was lovely and chilled just the way she liked it. Barbara soon finished cooking and brought breakfast over. It looked great: Barbara had cooked a full English breakfast. Katie and Barbara sat at the table and ate their breakfast. Afterward, Barbara made a pot of tea.

"Okay, Katie, so what do you want to talk about?"

"Oh, I am going to ask Roy for a divorce!"

"That's a huge step. Are you sure?"

"I have never been more, sure of anything, I am scared though."

"Okay, does Joshua know? Is this because you two have been getting close?"

"No, I don't want Joshua to think this is because of him: it's not. It's because I want to live my life free from Roy. I don't want to be married to him: I want to be Katie Maddison again. Also, I think it will help Roy accept I am serious about not returning. I am going ask for my horse Katherine, too, I don't want to leave her with Roy."

"I think it's good for you. Then you can truly have a fresh start. There is plenty of room for Katherine in the stables. So that's not a problem. "

"I do think that at some point you need to tell Joshua. How do think Roy is going to take it?"

"In a word, badly. That is one of the reasons why I wanted to tell you before I did it. His temper is terrible, and I have no idea what he will do. But I am going to tell him today. I plan to tell Joshua tomorrow after it's done" Katie said.

"Okay, well you know you have my full support. I do think it's best to get it over with" Barbara replied.

"Thank you, Barbara, it means a lot" Katie said, as she reached for the teapot in the middle of the table.

"Right, one more cup of tea and I will go call him" Katie said.

"I am starting to think that. I should have made Irish Coffee instead."

"No, save that for, after the call. I think I will need it."

"Good luck, Katie!" Barbara said.

Katie finished her tea and slowly made her way upstairs. She grabbed her phone and sat on the bed. She paused, for a minute and took a deep breath.

You can do this Katie, It's, just a phone call he can't hurt you over the phone!

Katie dialed his number slowly and listened to the phone ring three times before he answered. Those rings seemed to last forever.

"Katie! Unless you have come to your senses. I have nothing to say to you" Roy said.

"Roy! Listen to me. We need to talk" Katie replied.

"Fine. I'm listening."

"I am not coming back. I want you to send me Katherine. And then I want a divorce!"

"Did you fall and bump your head? I am not doing either. Divorce, indeed! Have you any idea how that would make me look?"

"Frankly, I don't care how it makes you look. I want a divorce, I no longer want to be your wife. I am staying in Texas, and I am going to build a new life for myself."

"Katie, I have tried to be patient with you. But you have gone too far. I will give you one last chance to come home right away and stop this nonsense."

"No! It's not nonsense. I will never come back to you. I want a divorce and even if I must save every penny to pay for it. I am going to get one. I also want my horse. I could never be your wife again."

"Let me make this clear. Katie! I will destroy your life and everyone in it. Then I will Kill you! I would do all this before I would divorce you or send you your precious horse."

Tears started streaming down Katie's cheeks. She took a deep breath and said,

"Why do you have to be so difficult and cruel. Roy? We are getting divorced, and I suggest you get used to the idea. And I will fight for Katherine through the solicitors."

"You wouldn't live long enough to Katie!"

"Don't threaten me! I am not scared of you anymore."

"Well, you should be scared, very scared. My temper is worse than the devil himself, and you are about to find out how bad it can actually get!"

Katie ended the call. Tears streamed down her cheeks. She threw herself on the bed and sobbed till the pillow was soaked through.

He couldn't kill me! He's not that crazy, surely.

Katie went into the bathroom and washed her face. She looked in the mirror as she dried her face. It was all blotchy. Katie took a deep breath and went downstairs to tell Barbara what had happened.

As she reached the bottom step, Barbara said,

"Oh! Katie! Whatever is wrong?"

"It was horrible, Barbara. He refused to give me a divorce and refused to give me Katherine. He said he was going kill me! And that he would destroy my life and everyone in it before he gave me a divorce."

"Katie, it will be okay, we will go see a solicitor tomorrow. And I will call John MacAulay this evening to alert the police about his threats. I doubt they will come to anything, he's just trying to bully and scare you."

"Oh! Do you really think so, Barbara?"

"Yes, it will all be fine. Besides, I would never let anyone hurt you. Come and have some coffee."

"Okay!"

Katie brushed the tears from her eyes and sat down on the sofa. Katie took the mug of coffee Barbara offered her and started to sip it.

"Thank you, Barbara, I don't know how I would cope without you sometimes."

"That's sweet, I will always be here for you. You should know that."

"I know. This coffee is really good."

"Thanks. I am glad you like it."

"I could just sit here all day."

"We could do that. I will get some movie's out, and we can have a slumber day."

"Oh, great idea."

Katie cuddled on the sofa and waited for Barbara to return. When she did, they watched a pile of romantic comedy films, until, finally, Katie fell asleep. Barbara got a blanket, put it over Katie, went upstairs to phone John, the police chief, and tell him what had been said.

"Hello, John!" Barbara said.

"Hello, Barbara! What can I do for you?"

"We have a situation. Katie called her husband today to ask for a divorce and her horse, and, well, he threatened to kill her."

"Really? Is he known to be violent?" John asked.

"He hit Katie. It's part of the reason she came to see me. I am not sure whether he was just trying to scare her or is actually planning something, but I thought it best to report it" Barbara replied.

"Okay, I will make the other officers aware, and come and see you and Katie in the morning. If anything happens in the meantime, call me right away. Best to treat this as serious until we know otherwise. How's Katie holding up? It must have been a shock!"

"She is resting downstairs on the sofa."

"Probably best, all right. I will see you first thing!"

"Thanks John."

"You're welcome Barbara."

Barbara went back downstairs and she sat on the chair while Katie slept.

Chapter 23

Meanwhile, in Cornwall, Roy put his phone down and then threw it in the fire. He watched the flames roar and rise as the drink disappeared. Roy was furious, he had never been so mad. He had always been the one who made demands. No one had ever dared ask anything of him. His wrath was well known in Cornwall.

How dare she demand a divorce and her horse? I gave her that horse. What makes her think she has any right at all to that horse, I paid for it. She is my possession and mine alone and all that she has belongs to me. No, she won't stay in Texas. I won't allow it. Time to teach Katie a lesson, and I will start with that horse.

Roy stormed through the castle grounds with his fury getting stronger and stronger as he did. He hit anything that got in his way. He didn't stop or blink until he reached the stables. Filled with an uncontrollable rage that illuminated his face.

His wild hair blowing about. Once inside the stables that housed Katie's horses, his rage grew.

I will kill that horse. Yes, I will make it suffer and so make Katie suffer. I am sure Anna will fill her in on the details. Now what to use?

The rage inside him created a tight knot in his stomach. He had gone way past reason. The staff came to see what he wanted.

"I want everybody out, everyone but Anna!" he said.

"Me. Sir?" Anna asked. She was shaking to her core, she was terrified.

The staff left, one by one. Clarissa left but waited nearby for Anna. She was scared for her friend. Although she had seen Roy in a mood before. This was something different, something darker.

Roy grabbed Anna's arm and threw her into the corner.

"Please, sir, what did I do?" Anna cried.

"You're friends with my wife! Are you not?"

"Well. Yes, sir, I still don't understand what I did wrong!"

"You will witness this, and you can report back to pretty little Katie, that's your purpose!" Roy said.

Anna froze in the corner; she had no idea what was about to happen. She was frozen in fear. She watched as Roy took the pitchfork from the door of the stables. Katherine was lying down in her stall Roy walked towards her with the pitchfork in both hands gripping it tight. As he raised the pitchfork up in the air above Katherine.

"Sir! No, you can't!" Anna screamed.

Roy brought the fork crashing down into Katherine's throat.

"Oh. But you see I did" Roy said, as he calmly walked out.

The horse was thrashing about, screaming in agony. Anna was frozen in fear; she had no idea what to do. Katherine had blood trickling out now.

Anna finally managed a scream, and Clarissa came running to her aid.

Clarissa saw Katherine bleeding on the hay with the fork still lodged in her throat.

“Oh my god. Come on, let’s get you out of here,” Clarissa said.

Anna clung to Clarissa as they left the stables. Once outside, Anna turned around to see the castle engulfed in flames.

“Look, the castles on fire!” Anna said.

Clarissa turned around to seeAnna was right.

“He’s lost his mind, we got to get away from here,” Clarissa said.

“But there are people in there!” Anna replied.

"Let's get to the main road. We can call for help from there!"

Anna and Clarissa ran to the main road, which was a safe distance from the fire. Anna dropped on the ground in a heap.

"You all right?" Clarissa asked.

"What kind of a monster is he? To take an innocent animals' life like that. I just don't understand!"

"I know, but Anna, I need you to focus right now, we need to call for help and then get the hell out of here."

"I'll try" Anna said.

Clarissa took out her phone and dialed emergency services.

"We need help! The castle in St Just is on fire. There are people in there!"

"Okay, I need you to stay calm, where are you," the voice on the other end said

“On the main road, but we can’t stay here. Mr. Kyle, he’s gone crazy. He set fire to everything, the castle and the stables. All the staff are in there.”

“Okay! I going to send emergency services there.”

Clarissa hung up.

“Right. Come on, Anna. Let’s get you home,” Clarissa said.

Clarissa walked Anna home as quickly as Anna could manage. Anna lived in a little cottage on the outskirts of St Just. The cottage left to her when her parents had died. Clarissa sat her down in a chair and put a blanket around her.

“I am going to make you a drink, you need something for the shock!” Clarissa said.

“Okay!” Anna replied.

Clarissa was back soon with a whiskey in one hand and warm sweet tea in the other.

"Drink this first," Clarissa said, handing Anna the whiskey.

Anna took the glass and threw the liquid down her throat. She could feel it burn as it slowly went down.

"Now, this!" Clarissa said, passing her the tea.

Anna took the tea in her trembling hands and took a sip. Clarissa put the television on and turned to the news. She figured the news has reported the fire by then. And sure, enough, they were. The fire crew and ambulances had arrived at the scene. Clarissa turned off the sound.

"I need to call home!" Clarissa said, as she disappeared into the bedroom. She called her parents and explained she was safe but needed to stay with Anna for at least the night as she was in shock.

"Oh, Katie," Anna said.

"What about Katie? She's in Texas?" Clarissa said.

"I have to tell her because, he said so. That's why he made me watch!"

"Oh my god! Are you serious?"

"Yes! He's going to her next. I have to call Katie. Clarissa."

"Okay, use my phone, and call her."

Clarissa dialed the number Anna told her as Anna was still shaking badly. Clarissa passed the phone to Anna.

"Katie! It's Anna!"

"Anna! What's wrong?" Katie asked.

"It's Mr. Kyle. He went crazy, and I am sorry so sorry, but he killed Katherine. Katie! He made me watch."

Anna was crying hysterically now.

"He what? Killed Katherine? How? When?"

"Earlier. He put a pitchfork in her throat. Katie, it was horrible, he set fire to everything afterward, the staff were inside, he burned the castle."

"I think I am going to be sick! What have I done?" Katie said.

Tears were streaming down Katie's cheeks.

"Katie! You must stay away forever. Promise me you will stay away from him!" Anna said.

"I promise, Anna. Be careful, please. There no telling what he will do if he has lost his mind."

"I will. Katie! Bye."

Katie put the phone down.

"What's going on?" Barbara asked.

"I..., I need a computer I need to check the news in Cornwall."

Barbara passed Katie her laptop and Katie sat at the table and googled the news in St Just. It was reported as a live event, the castle was still burning and eight people were dead with five more injured. Katie closed the laptop and fell into the chair.

"Katie!" Barbara said.

"What have I done? He has lost his mind, he killed my horse, murdered her. Then he set fire to the castle and stables with everyone inside. That death count is going to rise."

"Oh, Katie! I don't know what to say, he's a monster."

"You're right. He is, and I should have known that"

"Oh, Katie!"

"Barbara. I have to go lie down."

Katie walked slowly and calmly up to her room and shut the door behind her. She threw herself on the bed and cried until she fell asleep. It was too much for Katie to cope with.

Chapter 24

Barbara was sitting downstairs on the sofa when there was a knock on the door.

"Hello, Barbara!" John said.

"Hello, John! Come on in," Barbara said.

"Is Katie home?"

"She is upstairs sleeping, she had quite the shock"

"Yes, I had a call from England. The police are trying to locate her. They mentioned something about a fire!"

"Yes, have a cup of tea while I fill you in!"

"Thank you!"

"Katie got a call this afternoon from Cornwall. Apparently, her husband Roy, has gone crazy. He killed Katie's favorite horse and then set fire to the castle they lived in. We looked it up, the fire looked bad. People died."

"Do you know where he is?" John asked.

"No. No idea!" Barbara said.

"I see."

"You, don't think he would come here, do you?"

"No telling. If, he does he has lost his mind."

"I haven't even considered that. What should we do?"

"I will handle it. I will put a trace on his mobile phone, so we can track him. I am afraid I need to see Katie. I need to confirm her presence here for the authorities."

"I will wake her, but she's quite distraught."

Barbara went upstairs and gently woke Katie up.

"I am sorry, sweetie, but John, the police chief, is downstairs. He needs to see you, so he can confirm to the authorities that, you're here and well."

"Oh, Okay I will be right down."

Katie washed her face, fixed her clothes, and went downstairs.

"Hello, John!" Katie said.

"Hello Katie! I am so sorry, I just needed to see you in person."

"I understand."

"Well, I will go and leave you ladies in peace."

"Thank you, John. I will see you out," Barbara said.

Katie lay on the sofa and curled up in a ball.

"Katie, I'm so sorry about Katherine. Would you like anything? Can I do anything?" Barbara asked.

"No, thank you. I think I am going to go back to bed now," Katie replied.

"I will see you a bit later."

Katie returned to her room, lay on the bed, and started crying again. She cried herself to sleep. Katie didn't leave her room for two days. After that, she went only to eat or to sit silently with Goliath in his stables. It was comforting to her somehow. Katie couldn't talk to anyone. She was still crying herself to sleep every night. There was nothing anyone could do or say to help, so her friends just watched painfully as Katie struggled to come to terms with what had happened. Katie never went anywhere but college. She was polite to people but avoided eye contact and conversation.

It had been two weeks since the events in Cornwall. Katie still a shell of her former self. She still blamed herself for what had happened. Joshua and Barbara were very worried. Katie would eat maybe one meal a day. They were starting to wonder if she would ever be herself again. Joshua stopped by every day after work to ask Barbara how Katie was? Today Joshua had an idea, as he walked in, he said.

"Hi, Barbara!"

"Hi, Joshua!"

"I've been thinking about Katie. I thought I would take her for a walk by the river to get her out the house for a while."

"You can only try. I don't know if she will go. She's still quite withdrawn," Barbara said.

"I will go talk to her. Is she upstairs?"

"Yeah."

"Okay, see you in a minute."

Joshua walked upstairs and knocked on Katie's door.

"Yes," Katie sighed.

"It's Joshua! Can I come in?"

"I suppose so," Katie said.

"Hi, Katie!"

"Hi, Joshua! How can I help you?"

"Well, you could start with a shower. You stink!"

"I am not in the mood for jokes."

"Good, I wasn't joking."

"Don't be mean!"

"I am not. Listen, I know you're struggling with things, and it's not surprising, but I think it would do you good to get out of this room for a while. I thought I could take you down by the river."

"Oh, Joshua, it's a sweet idea, but I am not sure."

"Listen, Katie, I just want to help. You can just sit there and watch the water and the sunset. You don't even have to talk unless you want to."

"Just give me a few minutes."

"I will be downstairs waiting."

Katie got showered and changed while Joshua waited downstairs.

Best get this over with. I don't feel like going out, but maybe Joshua is right. It might be good for me.

Katie slowly made her way downstairs.

"Hello, Katie!" Barbara said. Shocked Joshua had managed to get Katie to leave her room.

"Hello, Barbara! I am going for a walk with Joshua; I won't be long."

"Okay, Katie. Take your time!"

"Come on. Katie. Let's go," Joshua said

Katie quietly followed Joshua out, Barbara smiled at her as she left. Barbara was relieved that Katie was spending time outside.

If anyone can get through to Katie, it's going to be Joshua.

Joshua walked straight down to the river; it was deserted. Katie sat on the bank. Joshua followed her and sat next to her.

Best to just sit here and see if she talks.

An hour passed. Katie was just sat there quietly, running her fingers through the grass.

"Whenever you want to go back, Katie, just let me know."

"Actually, I like being here watching the water."

"Oh, okay."

"You all think I'm being silly, don't you?" Katie asked.

"Katie, no one's thinking that. I promise, people are just concerned about you, that's all. What he's done is terrible. No-one should have to deal with that."

"Thank you. You're very kind, Joshua."

"I mean every word."

"Maybe, this is what I deserve."

"For what? Daring to have a life? Seriously he did what he did to hurt people, to hurt you. This is not your fault Katie. Don't you dare blame yourself for this. There was no way to know he would do this."

“I just keep thinking that I could have changed it somehow.”

“Oh, Katie, if you had been there you would likely be dead too. It’s not worth thinking about.”

“I guess.”

“You know I’m right. I am always right,” Joshua said.

“Can your head get any bigger?” Katie asked.

“I will let you know.”

“Can we go back now?”

“Sure, let’s go.”

Joshua took Katie back to the house and she returned straight to her room and shut the door.

“Well, I am impressed,” Barbara said.

“About what?” Joshua asked.

“Well that you got her to go out of the house.”

“Yeah, I have magical powers, don’t you know?”

"You wish Joshua, but thank you."

"No worries. I'll see you tomorrow."

"Bye, Joshua!"

Chapter 25

Meanwhile back in Cornwall, Michael was growing concerned about Roy's whereabouts. He had completely disappeared. Michael had asked around, but no-one had seen him. The details of the fire were now clearer. The authorities said it was deliberate, but they were still unclear of the motive or suspect. Twenty-one people had died in the fire with fifteen more injured in hospital. The castle and the stables were destroyed, and what was left had been demolished into a pile of rubble because of safety concerns.

Michael concerns were two-fold. Mainly, he was concerned because Roy was his friend and he was worried about his health and state of mind, wherever he was. But, secondly, Roy was also his Landlord. And with Katie still gone it was unclear what would happen with his tenancy. And Michael had never been very nice to Katie. In fact, he hated Katie and had made sure she was aware of the fact.

Determined to track Roy down, Michael realized he needed help, he needed someone people would talk to. As it was well known that Michael was Roy's best friend, no-one, would talk to him. People in St Just were very tight-lipped in times of trouble.

I will have to talk to Anna. She's the only one left nice enough, for people to talk to and that I can manipulate into helping me. The stupid girl will believe anything I tell her.

St Just was the kind of town where everyone knows where everyone else lived. In fact, it was the kind of place where everyone knew everything about everyone. So, Michael took a walk over to Anna's house.

Anna and Clarissa sat in the house, having a cup of tea. Clarissa had been staying close ever since the fire. Suddenly there was a knock at the door.

Clarissa answered the door.

"Hello, Michael!" Clarissa said.

"Hello. Is Anna home? I wanted to check to see if she's, all right?" Michael asked.

"Hold on," Clarissa said.

Clarissa shut the door, turned around and asked Anna,

"It's Michael to see you. Do you want me to let him in?"

"Yes, of course," Anna said.

Clarissa opened the door.

"Come in," she said.

"Thank you," Michael said.

"Hello, Michael!" Anna said.

"Anna! Thank goodness, you're all right," Michael said.

"Well, I'm alive. I'm, not so sure about anything else," Anna said.

"Anna, I'll be in the kitchen," Clarissa said.

"I heard about the fire. Well, everyone has. I have been trying to find out what happened, but people aren't really talking about it," Michael said.

"Michael, I am not really surprised," Anna said.

"I don't understand."

"You're Roy's best friend! Why would people talk to you after what he did?"

"That's the thing, Roy disappeared too. I have been trying to find him, but I have had no luck."

"Good, I hope he stays gone. You realize this is his doing, right?"

"What? No, Anna, he wouldn't."

"Sit, down, and let me tell you what happened."

"Please do. I am so confused."

"He went crazy. I mean he went completely out of his mind. He ordered everyone out of the stables, but me. He...."

Anna took a deep breath, tears running down her cheeks. She continued.

"He murdered Katie's horse, Katherine. He told me I had to watch so I could tell Katie she is next. Then he went and burned the castle down."

"Oh, Anna, I am so sorry. That sounds unbearable," Michael said, before walking over and giving Anna a big hug.

"Thank you, but that's why no-one will talk to you."

"I am in shock. I don't know what to think. Do you know what happened to make him that crazy?"

"Honestly no, but I am glad he's gone. I hope he never comes back."

"I understand, but I have to find him before he does any more damage. He needs to face up to what he's done and deal with the consequences. The thing is, I need help."

"Help? What kind of help."

"Just someone, people will talk to, so I can track him down. Once I find him. I will make him turn himself into the authorities."

"I see, I just don't want to ever have to ever hear his name or think about this anymore. I have nightmares every night about what happened."

"I would never forgive myself if he hurt anyone else. And what if he hurt Katie? I don't think I could live with myself."

"I hadn't thought of that. I couldn't bear it if anything happened to Katie. Okay I will help if I can!"

"No, Anna, don't you dare!" Clarissa said storming out from the kitchen.

"Clarissa, I don't want Roy back in St. Just either. But it's the right thing to do," Anna said.

"Then I am leaving I won't have any part in this. Anna," Clarissa said, and she left, pushing Michael out of the way as she passed him.

"I will see what I can find out and call you," Anna said.

"Thank you. Anything you need, call me. I will check in on you every evening."

"Does Katie know about all this?" Michael asked.

"Yes, I called her. I will keep in touch with her and see if she has any news," Anna answered.

"Thank you, so much. My number is 079-555-4666. Remember, call me if you need anything. I am going to go home. But I will check on you tomorrow."

"Okay, Michael see you tomorrow," Anna said.

Michael left, and Anna programmed his number into her phone and went to lie down. It was the first time Anna had been alone since the fire. But it was nice and somehow, peaceful.

I will go catch up on the gossip tomorrow.

It wasn't long before Anna fell asleep.

In Texas, Katie had seemed a little brighter since her time out with Joshua. Barbara was very grateful. The following week, Katie went back to work, attended college, and did well in her class. Katie still wasn't eating much or talking much, but she was up and about, which was an improvement. Every few days, Joshua would drive Katie to a relaxing space, she would talk a little about how she was feeling, and he would take her home. It seemed to help.

Barbara felt a little helpless, because she couldn't do anything for Katie, but as Katie was getting back to her usual self. Barbara and Katie slowly spent more time together.

Chapter 26

Back in, Cornwall. Michael had tracked Roy down to a Hotel in Central London. By tracking his credit card online. He had packed some clothes in an overnight bag and decided to go and see Anna to see whether she had any information for him. Michael drove over to Anna's house.

Michael knocked on Anna's door.

"Hello, Anna!" he said, when she opened the door.

"Hello, Michael, would you like to come in?" Anna answered.

"Thank you!" Michael said, stepping inside.

"I wasn't expecting you," Anna said.

"Sorry, I should have called first, it's just I found out where Roy is. He's in London!"

"Oh!" Anna said.

“I am going to go see if I can convince him to hand himself into the authorities.”

“To London?” Anna asked.

“Yes, he’s not answering his phone and it is probably best face to face,” Michael replied.

“Oh, I see. So, you came to say goodbye.”

“Just to let you know, I was going.”

“Well, have a safe trip,” Anna said.

“Have you heard from Katie?”

“No! I haven’t heard anything. So, are you going to bring Roy back here? Anna asked.

“Hopefully he will go to the police station right away after that who knows,” Michael replied.

“Okay, well keep me informed please, I really don’t want to come face to face with him”

“I’ll call while,I am away Anna!”

"Thank you!"

Michael turned towards the door, and Anna watched him leave, before, shutting the door again.

Anna sank into her sofa.

I wish he wasn't going! It's been so nice having him visit. It's lonely without Clarissa and I don't think she will ever visit me again, she's so angry about me trying to help Michael. Once he finds Roy, I doubt I will see Michael again. I hope and pray Roy doesn't return to St Just I don't know what I would do? Move maybe?

Chapter 27

In Texas, Katie had finished her course and passed with impressive results. Barbara was busy planning a party to celebrate Katie passing her course. Joshua was feeling insecure about his feelings for Katie. He decided to go and talk to Bryan.

Joshua drove up to Bryan's farm after work one evening. He knocked on the door, and Bryan answered.

"It's Joshua!" Bryan shouting inside to his parents as he left.

"Hey, Bryan!" Joshua said.

"Hey, Joshua! what's wrong?"

"Nothing! I just thought I would come by!"

"Let's go down to the bottom field."

"Okay."

"Somethings wrong. What is it?"

"Katie!"

"Katie?"

"I've been spending lots of time with her. You know, because of everything she's going through."

"Well, I did hear the rumors; you know what it's like around here. Are they true?"

"If you mean, that he murdered her favorite horse, and burned the castle down. Yeah."

"Must have been terrible for her."

"Yes, it was, but that's not the problem."

"What is it then? Whatever it is it can't be that bad."

"I'm starting to really like her. I feel so much closer to her now."

"And that's a problem?"

“Yeah. I mean I’ve always liked her a bit, but she’s married. I am not good enough for her, and no one will accept it,” Joshua said.

“You both like each other, I saw that kiss. And no-one really cares mate. And nothing has happened you’re worrying for nothing trust me!”

“Thanks, Bryan.”

“I think it’s just all the time you spend together, and you were already getting close.”

“Thanks, mate. You’re right, I guess.”

“What do you mean you guess? I am always right. Want to come in the house? I want a cup of tea.”

“You wish, you were always right. Yeah, tea sounds good.”

Joshua followed Bryan into the house and stayed for a cup of tea before heading home.

The following morning at Barbara's, Katie was up early. Barbara was making tea and toast.

"You, got any plans today, Katie?" Barbara asked.

"I actually thought I would take Goliath for a ride. It's been a while since I have been riding."

"Sounds good! I have to pop into Houston to check on a few things for the party."

"Oh Barbara, do you mind if I tag along. I need a new dress, I'd forgotten the party is tomorrow."

"Yeah, well I am going this morning. So, you could come to Houston and go riding later?"

"Great! I'll just get ready."

Katie disappeared up the stairs to go change.

"Morning, Barbara!" Joshua said as he walked in.

"Morning, Joshua!"

"Anything, I need to know before I start work?"

"Not really. I am going to Houston to check a few things for tomorrow. Katie's coming with me, and, oh, she wants to go riding on Goliath later so can you make sure Bryan knows to have him ready."

"No problem. It's good she's going riding again. I will see you later."

Katie came down the stairs.

"Morning, Katie!" Joshua said.

"Morning, Joshua!" Katie said.

Joshua left the house.

"Something, I said?" Katie asked.

"No, he was on his way out anyway," Barbara said.

"You ready?"

"Yeah, let's go."

Once in Houston, Katie and Barbara hit every clothes shop they could find to search for Katie's perfect new dress. Katie ended up choosing a light pink, shirt dress with a black belt. She also got black calf length boots to complete the outfit. Barbara chose a white shift dress with white sandals. Barbara and Katie visited the catering company to double check the menu for tomorrow and the bakers to drop off the cake stand before having lunch and returning home.

Barbara and Katie were just sitting down in the living room and drinking tea when Joshua came in.

"Hi, Barbara!" he said.

"Hello, Joshua!" Barbara said.

"Hi, Katie! Bryan says Goliath is ready whenever you are," Joshua said.

"Hi, Joshua! great," Katie said.

Katie finished her tea and went upstairs to get ready to go riding. Joshua watched Katie walk upstairs and smiled.

"Erm! I saw that," Barbara said and laughed

“I don’t know what you are talking about. Barbara,” Joshua said.

“Of course, you don’t. I’m watching you.”

“You always are!”

“Ready,” Katie said as she came back downstairs.

“Great! I will walk you down to the stables,” Joshua said.

Katie and Joshua left together. Barbara laughed and shook her head.

Those two are so going end up together.

Katie and Joshua walked down towards the stables, Joshua left as they reached the stable door.

Katie walked in the stables and toward Bryan.

“Katie! You all right?” Bryan said.

“I’m great! Thanks. How are you?” Katie asked.

“I’m good. Thank you.”

“I’m going to take Goliath, for a ride.”

“Yes, he’s allready and waiting.”

“Great! I’ll see you in a while then.”

“Yeah, I will be around.”

“Hiya, boy! Sorry, it’s been a while,” Katie said to Goliath.

Katie mounted Goliath and left. Goliath trotted slowly out of the stables. Katie headed straight for a country lane and went out of town.

It feels so good to be out riding again.

Katie and Goliath picked up speed as they headed out of town and deep into the countryside. Katie loved it when Goliath was galloping fast. She liked her hair blowing in the wind. It made her feel free, wild and unstoppable. Katie turned into a deserted, dusty back road and let Goliath go as fast as he wanted. It was good for him to have a good run now and again. After a while, they detoured into an open field and sat down on the grass.

"I love you, Goliath. You're the best horse. Of, courseI loved Katherine too, but it was different. It is weird knowing that she's gone. I think you would have liked her if you had ever met."

Katie remounted and they headed back slowly with, the sun beating down on them. They went slowly, Katie was enjoying the countryside as they went home. Back at the stables, Bryan asked.

"Did you have fun?"

"Yes, as always, he is going to need water. We went right out of town and it's so hot now."

"No, problem. Katie."

"I'll see you tomorrow at the party. You are coming, right?"

"Yes, I wouldn't miss it for the world."

"Great, see you then."

"Bye, Katie!"

Katie made her way up to the house. She was exhausted now and just wanted to relax.

I just want to lie on the sofa with some lemonade.

"Hello, Katie, did you have a nice ride?" Barbara asked

"Hello, Barbara! Yes, it was lovely. It's really hot outside now, and I'm exhausted."

"Sit down, and I'll bring you some lemonade."

"It's like you read my mind. Thanks!"

"You're welcome."

"It was good to be out riding a horse again."

"Yes, it's very therapeutic."

"How was your day?"

"It was good, but I think a movie and relaxing on the sofa is all I'll being doing this evening."

"How about you?"

"You know, Barbara. I think, I will join you. We could order pizza."

"Great idea."

"Katie continued sitting on the sofa. She was happy to just be resting a relaxing evening was just what she needed. Katie and Barbara enjoyed an evening full of movies, pizza. and lounging on the sofa, before finally going to bed.

Chapter 28

The following day, Katie slept in while Barbara finished her last-minute preparations for Katie's party. Although the guest list was short the theme and decorations were as large as ever. Barbara had gone with the theme of a festival, and everything was starting to come together. All the rosettes were pink, cerise and white with 'Well Done Katie' in the middle in gold writing. They had been delivered to all the guests to wear. The entrance to the bottom field had been draped in pink, cerise, and white silk bunting and a large 'Well Done Katie' sign. There were stalls set up with different activities, archery and lucky horseshoes. The catering trucks were starting to arrive. There was an ice sculpture of a horse, and balloons everywhere. There was even a cotton candy store. Barbara had set up hay bales to sit on for groups of three. Barbara was sure Katie would love it. After Katie's hard work and all she had been through, she deserved the best party Barbara could give her, and this was it.

Barbara returned to the house around lunchtime. Katie sat in a pair of leggings and a t-shirt with her hair up, drinking coffee.

"Hello, Katie! Have you just got up?" Barbara asked.

"Hello, Barbara! Yes, not long ago."

"I was just checking on the preparations for later."

"Oh, how's it all looking?"

"Good. It's all on schedule."

"Great! I am looking forward to it."

"Yeah, it should be a great night."

"Is Joshua coming?"

"I think so. Have you not seen him?"

"No, he's been a bit distant in, the last couple of days."

"What have you done?"

"Nothing. Why don't you ask what he's done? It's not like he's perfect or something."

"It's not that. It's just, well, it's plain to see that Joshua adores you. So, it's more likely he's in a mood over something you said or done. That's all."

Joshua adores me that's good to know

A smile slowly spread across Katie's face.

"What is that smile, for?" Barbara said.

"No, nothing, honestly," Katie replied.

"Really?"

"Yes, it's going to be great to see everyone later."

"Don't change the subject, Katie."

"What? I 'm not. It will be. Are you not looking forward to seeing everyone?"

"Yes, I am. Not as much as I am looking forward to a long bath."

"Well! You have plenty of time, before the party!"

"Yeah! I am going to go get a bath now!"

"See you in a while, Barbara."

Katie turned around on the sofa and cuddled a cushion. As she put her feet up on the sofa,

Joshua walked in.

"Someone looks comfy!" he said.

"Yeah, I am," Katie said.

"Good."

"I was just asking Barbara, are you coming tonight to my party?"

"Of, course. I wouldn't miss it for the world."

"Funny, that's exactly what Bryan said."

"I will be there. The field looks great. This may be Barbara's best party yet!"

"Great!"

"Did you want Barbara? She has just gone for a bath."

"Nothing that won't wait, see you later, Katie."

"See you later, Joshua."

Katie turned around and snuggled into the sofa. She watched tv for a little while. Later, Barbara came downstairs.

"Did I hear Joshua, earlier?" Barbara asked

"Yes, you did. He says it's nothing that can't wait," Katie replied.

"Okay. Do you want a cup of tea, Katie?"

"Oh, yes, please. Barbara."

Barbara brought the tea over and sat on the sofa with Katie. After a little while, Barbara said.

"I am going to check that everything is ready: people will be arriving soon."

Katie was downstairs, drinking lemonade when Barbara returned with Joshua.

“You look lovely, Katie!” Barbara said.

“Yes, beautiful as always,” Joshua said.

“Thank you, Barbara! Thanks, Joshua!” Katie said.

“Right then! I will just go and get changed, and we will be ready to go,” Barbara said.

Five minutes later. She was ready and all three of them headed down to the party in the bottom field.

“Oh! Barbara! You have out done yourself. This is great,” Katie gasped.

“Thank you. It has come together pretty great.”

“I am going to get a drink,” Joshua said, walking away.

“Katie!” shouted Cordy, running toward her and giving her a hug.

“Hello, Cordy!” Katie said, a little shocked at her excitement.

"It's good to see you again, this party is amazing."

"It's good to see you too. Cordy! We have Barbara to thank for the party! I can't take credit for that."

"Barbara, it's simply delightful," Cordy said.

"Thank you, Cordy! That's very kind," Barbara said.

"Come on, Katie I want to show you the ice sculpture."

"Go, on, Katie. I have to greet the guests," Barbara said.

"Okay, Cordy, let's go," Katie said.

Cordy led Katie to an ice sculpture of a horse. It was four feet tall and amazingly detailed.

"Isn't it great, Katie? Did you ever see anything like it?" Cordy asked.

"No! Never! It's wonderful!" Katie answered.

I can't believe how much the sculpture looks like Katherine!

"Hi, Katie!" Lynette said, as she approached Katie and Cordy.

"Hi, Lynette! How have you been?" Katie said.

"I'm good, thanks. Katie! Isn't this party great? Barbara is so clever," Lynette said.

"Yes, she is!" Katie answered.

"I am just going to go and get a drink," Katie said, as she turned to walk away.

It's nice to have something happy and positive to concentrate on.

Katie found the bar that had been set up. It wasn't really a bar, more of a table with enough equipment to make any drink. Katie saw Bryan and Joshua in the line, so she walked towards them.

"Hi, Bryan! Hi, Joshua!" Katie said.

"Hi, Katie! Are you having fun? The party is great, isn't it?" Bryan asked.

"Oh, yes. It's amazing."

"Hi, Katie!" Joshua said.

"Are you having fun?" Katie asked.

"Yes! What would you like to drink?" Joshua asked.

"Can I have blackcurrant and soda water, please?"

"Of, course. It's your party! You can have anything you want."

"Ooh! That's a point; I will have to remember that"

"Joshua! What have you done?" Bryan said, and laughed as he saw Katie's eyes light up.

Have anything I wonder, what is it that I want? Katie thought.

Bryan and Katie stepped away from the bar with their drinks.

"So, now that you finished your course! Katie! What do you think you will do next?" Bryan asked.

"Well, I thought. I would do the level two course. I am really interested in horse nutrition," Katie said.

"Really? You never mentioned that" Joshua said.

"Well, I don't tell you everything. Plus, you have been kind of busy lately."

"I am never too busy for you, Katie!" Joshua said.

"Don't be offended, Joshua. I haven't discussed it with Barbara yet either, or I have the whole summer to enjoy first. Level two doesn't start until September, and its only May," Katie said.

"Okay. I was just surprised!" Joshua said.

"Don't worry, Katie! Although Joshua doesn't gossip like the rest of us. He likes to think he knows everything about everybody," Bryan laughed.

"Yeah, I have noticed that. I am going to find Barbara," Katie said.

"She's welcoming the late arrivals by the gate!" Joshua said.

"Thank you, Joshua. See you later."

Katie walked away, slowly sipping her drink as she went.

Joshua watched Katie walk away.

Bryan laughed and said,

"Joshua, why don't you just, embrace the fact that you're crazy about her and tell her how you feel. I mean we all know she's crazy about you, too."

Joshua sighed.

"How do you know and who's 'we all,' Bryan?"

"It's just obvious!"

"Oh, right!"

"I'll see you later, Bryan!" Joshua said, as he walked away to go sit down.

Joshua shook his head.

Meanwhile, Katie had found Barbara by the gate.

"Hello, Barbara!" Katie said.

"Hello, Katie! Are you enjoying yourself?" Barbara asked.

"Oh yes. Everyone is commenting on what a great party this is. You have done an amazing job."

"Thank you. I just wanted you to have a good celebration. You have worked so hard and been through so much. I am very proud of you."

"Thank you, Barbara! Would you like me to get you anything?"

"That would be great. I would love some lemonade."

"I will be back in a minute."

Katie slowly walked away to go get Barbara a drink. Katie returned to Barbara fifteen minutes later with a plastic glass full of lemonade and a plate of fried chicken and onion rings.

"I thought you might like this, too," Katie said.

"Thank you, Katie. That is very thoughtful," Barbara said.

"You're welcome. It's the least I could do. I will see you a bit later."

Katie disappeared into the middle of the party again. Over the next few hours, Katie had a great time. She danced with her friends and ate the food, which was lovely. Katie loved fried chicken and onion rings. There were vodka jellies and rainbow-colored desserts which tasted like an instant pudding mix, and fresh cream strawberry tarts. Katie tried to spend a little bit of time with different groups of guests and posed for photos. Katie had a lot of strawberry wine. Katie didn't really drink much, she only had the occasional whiskey and wine. Drinking a glass of wine after a long day or with your evening meal had been a kind of religion in Cambridge, England where Katie grew up, so it was almost ingrained in her. Barbara made a speech. She thanked everyone for coming and told everyone how proud she was of Katie. Katie had said thank-you herself when she cut her cake. Katie's cake was huge. It was a big, white, square cake with white, pink, and purple piping and "Congratulations, Katie" was written in pink lettering. The cake was also topped with a champagne bottle and pink flowers, all covered in edible glitter. Katie had kept the flowers as a memory of the evening.

The sun had set, and the moon had come out. The moon was huge it owned the sky like a super moon. There was a sea of twinkling stars. The guests had started, to leave. Barbara, Joshua, and Bryan were saying goodbye to the leaving guests as Katie lay all curled up asleep on a hay bale in the middle of the field. When all the guests had left. Joshua walked over to Katie and gently tapped her on the shoulder.

"Come on, Katie time to go home!" Joshua said.

Katie woke up a yawned.

"Oh! Okay!" Katie said, wrapping her arms around Joshua's neck.

"Looks like, I am carrying her!" Joshua said handing Barbara, Katie's bag.

"Bryan! Can you carry Katie's cake back to the house, please?" Barbara asked.

"No problem, Barbara!" Bryan said.

Bryan picked up what was left of the cake, and Joshua scooped Katie up in his arms. They all walked up to the house. Joshua carried Katie into her room and lay her on the bed. She gently kissed him on the cheek as he put her down and fell asleep. Joshua made his way downstairs.

"Help yourself to cake and coffee! I am going to bed. Joshua be sure to lock up before you leave," Barbara said.

"I will. Good night," Joshua said.

Barbara went up to bed, and Bryan and Joshua got a slice of cake before locking the door as they left.

Chapter 29

Meanwhile, Michael had arrived at the hotel in London. He approached the front desk and said,

"Hello, I have come to see Roy Kyle. I believe he is staying here."

"I am sorry, Sir, but Mr. Kyle checked out this morning," the desk clerk said.

"Oh, I see. Do you have any idea where he went? It is very important that I talk to him as soon as possible."

"Hold on just a moment, sir," said the desk clerk, and he disappeared.

The desk clerk reappeared moments later with a door man.

"This is Justin, he drove Mr. Kyle this morning after he checked out," the desk clerk said.

"Hello, Justin!" Michael said politely.

“Hello, sir! I drove, Mr. Kyle to Heathrow Airport. He did say he was flying to New Jersey,” the doorman said.

“Thank you, very much. I don’t suppose he told you why,” Michael asked.

“No, Sir! He did not,” the doorman said

“Thank you. You have been very helpful,” Michael said and left.

Michael got back into his car and began to drive to the airport.

Why would he go to New Jersey of all places, Katie’s in Texas and New Jersey is not a usual transfer point on that route! Why wouldn’t he fly direct? What is he up to now!

When Michael finally got to the airport. He searched it frantically for any sign for Roy with no luck.

I really don’t want to go to New Jersey.

Michael tried Roy's phone and searched for Roy one more time before heading to the ticket desk.

"Hi, can a get a ticket on the next flight to New Jersey, please?" asked Michael handing the assistant his passport.

"Certainly, the next plane for New Jersey leaves in two hours. Would you like first class or economy seat," the assistant asked.

"First if possible, but if you get me on the plane. I don't really care," Michael said.

"One first class ticket to New Jersey leaving at 14:00 hours," said the assistant.

"Thank you!" Michael said, handing her his credit card.

Michael took the travel documents and checked in at the check in desk before sitting down to call Anna.

"Hello, Anna!" Michael said.

“Michael! I didn’t expect to hear from you! Did you find him?” Anna asked.

“No, I haven’t found him. I just missed him. He’s heading to New Jersey,” Michael said.

“Oh, Michael! Does that mean he’s going after Katie?” Anna asked.

“I don’t think, so. New Jersey doesn’t have many connections to Texas. There are faster ways to get there. Have you heard from Katie?” Michael asked.

“No, but I think I will phone have to phone her in a minute. Are you coming back?” Anna asked.

“That’s a good idea! She may know where he’s heading. I am going to New Jersey see if I can find him there. Keep in touch, Anna,” Michael said.

I need to find Roy! He’s a pain but he’s the only friend I have!

"Okay, Michael. I will," Anna said, before putting the phone down.

Michael walked over to get a coffee and a newspaper, before heading through security and to his departure longue.

Michael was soon in his first-class window seat on the plane to New Jersey.

When Michael arrived in New Jersey.

What on earth, am I going to do now. I only have the doorman's word that Roy has come here. How am I to find him before he moves on again.

Michael booked himself a room in the local hotel and decided to have some dinner before trying to further track Roy's movements via his credit card.

Chapter 30

Meanwhile back in Texas, it was the morning after the party. Katie and Barbara sat on the sofa with a cup of tea when the phone rang.

"Hello!" said Barbara.

"Hello, Barbara! It's John," the voice said.

"I need to talk to you and Katie!"

"Is it bad news?" Barbara asked, as Katie sat up.

I am not sure exactly. It is best that I stop by," John said.

"Okay, come right around!" Barbara said.

"I'll see you soon," John said.

Barbara put the phone down and said,

"John needs to talks to us! he's coming around."

"Is it about Roy?" Katie asked.

"I don't know," Barbara said.

Katie sat up. She was filled with dread. It was only about twenty minutes until John arrived, but it seemed like hours to Katie. Katie hadn't thought about Roy, with all the excitement of the party.

What if Roy is here already?

John walked straight in because the door was open. His usually friendly face looked stern and serious.

"It's Roy, isn't it?" Katie said.

"Yes, Katie! I am afraid so," John said.

Barbara passed John a cup of tea.

"I have been notified that Roy Kyle entered New Jersey today. He hasn't tried to book any other flights since he arrived, and we are still tracking him. Do you know why he would go to New Jersey?" John continued.

"No, I don't understand. I assumed if he came, he would come straight here," Katie said.

"Okay, I will keep you informed if we know anymore and try not to worry If he hires a car or tries to book a flight we will know immediately," John said.

"Thank you, John!" Barbara said.

John left, and Barbara saw him out. Katie pulled her feet up onto the sofa and cuddled into the side of the sofa.

What is he up to? Does he want me to drive myself crazy waiting for him to come and get me?

"I am going to make you a cup of tea. You need something sweet right now!" Barbara said.

"Can I have cake, too?"

"Of, course."

"He's coming after me, Barbara, I know he is. I can feel it."

"You can feel it?" Barbara asked.

"Yes, it's like an intense fear you can't shift, and your stomach begins to turn," Katie said.

Barbara handed Katie the cake and tea.

"All we know is he's in New Jersey. He won't get anywhere near here without the police tracking his every move."

Just then Katie's phone rang. Barbara and Katie looked at each other alarmed before Katie cautiously answered.

"Hello."

"Hi, Katie! It's Anna we need to talk," Anna said.

Katie put her hand on the phone and said to Barbara.

"It's Anna in Cornwall."

"Okay, Anna. What's going on?" Katie said, into the phone.

"Have you heard from Roy?"

"No. Please don't tell me you have another message, Anna."

"No, but he is in New Jersey."

"I know. How do you know that though?"

"Michael told me. Who told you, Katie?"

“The police. They are tracking him.”

“Oh, well. Michael has been tracking him, hoping he could talk some sense and get him to hand himself into the authorities.”

“Okay, Anna, listen to me. You can’t trust Michael he’s just as bad as Roy. Promise me you will stay away from him,” Katie said.

Anna sensed the fear and desperation in Katie’s voice.

“If it will make you feel better. He’s just trying to help he’s on his way to New Jersey as we speak.”

“Okay, I don’t trust Michael, and I never have. I mean, the man manipulates people for a living.”

“Oh! Katie! It’s just a job.”

“Anna, please be careful.”

“I will, Katie. I’ve got to go. I will call soon.”

Katie hung up the phone and took a big bite of the cake and a sip of tea.

"What's going on now?" Barbara asked.

"It seems, it's not just the authorities tracking Roy. His best friend Michael is tracking him and following him. Michael is on his way to New Jersey."

"Why?"

"I don't know. He gave Anna some story about trying to get Roy to hand himself in. But Michael is as bad as Roy, if not worse. He's never done anything without some dishonorable intention. Anna has a little crush on him, so he can wrap her around his little finger. Everyone in St Just knows about Anna's crush on him."

"Okay, I am going to go called John and tell him. Do you know Michael's last name? And what was that about his job?"

"Yes, it's Michael Dawson. He's a PR consultant, who lies for a living. He's really good at it too."

"Okay, I will be back soon," Barbara replied

Barbara went upstairs to give the new information to John, and Katie continued eating her cake and drinking her tea. Barbara reappeared moments later.

"John is going to track Michael too. We will sort this all out. He says to be very careful with what information you give Anna in the meantime."

"I intend to. Thanks. I want some more cake."

"Help yourself," Barbara laughed.

Katie and Barbara sit back down on the sofa.

"Are you okay, Katie? About all that's happening, I mean."

"I am scared. Roy's temper is so bad, and he's said he'd rather see me dead than divorce me!"

"I will make sure you're protected. And John will know the moment he tries to leave New Jersey."

"That's kind. Barbara, but I am not sure you can protect me. The fact he went to New Jersey itself is unexpected. He has no connections there that I know of."

"I guess we will have to wait it out and see what his next move is. I think I will go into town tomorrow and have a chat with John again to see if there's anything we can do to make you feel more secure. I would like you to stay close to Joshua while I am in town. It would just make me feel better."

"That's a good idea. It would make me feel better too."

"I bet. I will tell him in the morning. It will be good for you to learn what he actually does in a day," Barbara said.

"I know what he does all day, stares at me and talks to Bryan" Katie laughed.

"Katie! So, you noticed that, too."

"It's hard not to. I don't mind though. Don't tell him I have noticed Barbara."

"I won't. I'll leave you to do that."

Katie smiled and her face glow. It lit up at the thought of Joshua.

"See? It's not all bad Joshua's name still makes you smile," Barbara said.

"Yeah, true. I am going to go, lie down for a while," Katie said.

"Okay, I will see you later."

What can I do? I don't want Katie to feel scared! I mean, how bad is Roy's temper? I might have played it down until the fire and killing the horse. I mean what kind of monster kills an innocent animal to hurt someone. He says he loves.

Barbara decided to go through some invoices for the ranch she had been putting off, done. While Katie was sleeping best to keep occupied.

Chapter 31

The following morning, Katie and Barbara were both up early. They were grateful they had heard no more from John about Roy, which hopefully meant he had stayed in New Jersey at least last night. They were sitting at the table when Joshua walked in.

“Good morning, Barbara! Good morning, Katie!” Joshua said.

“Good morning, Joshua! Get a coffee, and come sit down,” Barbara said.

“What did I do?”

“Nothing. We just need to talk to you.”

Katie nodded at Joshua, while Barbara laughed.

Joshua cautiously walked over to the table and sat down.

“This is unnerving. Just tell me what it is?”

“Well, the thing is...” Barbara started.

"Barbara, let me tell him!" Katie said.

"Yes, can one of you please just tell me? it can't be that bad!"

"Well, depends on your definition of bad, really. John stopped by. Roy is in New Jersey," Katie said.

"Okay, just so I have got this straight. John MacAulay the police chief, has notified you that Katie's husband, Roy, is in New Jersey!" Joshua said, having a big sigh of relief. Joshua was relieved he hadn't done anything wrong.

"Yes!"

"So, why did you need to tell me? Is here coming here?"

"We hope not. No-one knows what Roy is up to, but as he wants me dead or home, John is tracking his movements," Katie said.

"Okay! Is there anything else?" Joshua asked.

“Yes, I am going into town to see John and I want you to keep an eye on Katie. So, she’s going to help you at work today,” Barbara said.

“Katie will help me do my job. Not a good idea!” Joshua said.

“Joshua, it isn’t a request. Katie is working with you today deal with it,” Barbara said.

“Fine. Well, don’t blame me if I don’t get anything done today.”

“Oh! Like you do any work anyway!” Katie said.

“Well, I am going to leave you to work this out. Have fun,” Barbara laughed.

“Bye, Barbara!” Katie said.

Barbara left, and as the door shut. Joshua rolled his eyes at Katie.

“Come on, let’s get this over with,” He said.

“Okay, if I have to,” Katie replied.

Katie stood behind Joshua and stopped at stared at his behind. Joshua turned around.

"What are you doing?" Joshua said.

"I'm being you. Yeah, that's right I have seen you," Katie replied.

"Have you now. So how come you are not working with Bryan today?"

"I think Barbara wanted me to feel safe and she thought you were the best person to look after me."

"Are you really shaken up over this Roy thing Katie?"

"I am scared. He's going to kill me. I know he will. It's just a matter of time."

"Oh, Katie, not while you're here he won't. We all adore you. People will keep you safe."

"That's not what I want. The last thing I want is for anyone else to get hurt."

“It is sweet that you don’t what anyone to get hurt. You’ll have to come help with the taking stock of the stable supplies. It is the most boring thing ever about an hour into this, you will wish you were dead, believe me.”

“That’s funny. Taking stock is not that bad. I have done it before,” Katie said.

Katie and Joshua headed to the stable stores, there were a few other people there. They all got to work. Katie worked alongside Joshua quietly. It took until lunchtime, but they managed to get all the work done, so Joshua was relieved.

“Are you heading to the house for lunch?” Joshua asked.

“Yes, I wanted to see if Barbara was back yet?” Katie replied.

“Okay, I will walk up with you.”

Joshua walked Katie back to the house, Barbara was home and had made lunch.

“Oh good. You didn’t kill each other,” Barbara said, when she saw them.

“No, still in one piece. I even managed to complete the stock take!” Joshua answered.

Katie was sat at the table, biting into a sandwich, when Barbara and Joshua turned to look at her.

“What, I didn’t get any breakfast,” Katie said, with her mouth full of food.

Barbara and Joshua sat, down and all three of them ate lunch together. When they were finished, Katie said.

“Barbara! Do you still need me to work with Joshua this afternoon?”

“That’s a good idea. I have a lot of stuff to take care of; I won’t be done until late tonight.”

“You’re really busy today? What are you up to?” Katie asked.

“Nothing, well nothing for you to worry about,” Barbara said.

"So, do I get any say in these work arrangements?" Joshua asked.

"No!" Katie and Barbara said together and then started laughing.

"Okay, come on, Katie. Let's see what trouble we can get into," Joshua said.

"Bye, Barbara!" Katie said.

"Oh, Joshua I need a word a minute."

"Okay, Katie, head down to the stables and I will meet you there."

Katie walked off in the direction of the stables.

"Now, I am having a meeting at the town hall about Katie and all this Roy business. Katie is feeling very insecure now."

"Yes, Barbara, she did mention she was worried."

"Yeah, I need you to keep her busy. Make sure she is okay while I am busy. I should be done about 7 p.m.."

“I will look after; don't worry.”

“Thanks, Joshua. I will see you later.”

Joshua went off to meet Katie at the stables and Barbara went back inside the house.

Chapter 32

It was 5:30 p.m. and Barbara had just arrived at the town hall. John and Susie MacAulay were helping her. Barbara was worried about how the townspeople would react to all the business with Roy. It was time to find out. All the chairs were laid out; the whole town had been invited. The people started to pour in, and the hall were soon full. John signaled for his deputy, Jason, to close the doors. Everyone was sitting down and chatting amongst themselves.

With Susie on one side and John on the other, Barbara took a deep breath. Susie put her hand on Barbara's shoulder.

"It's okay," she said.

"Thank you for coming, everyone," Barbara began.

"What's going on?" a voice from the crowd said.

"By now must of you have met Katie. Katie came here initially for a holiday, but she decided to stay and ask her husband in England for a divorce. He didn't take to kindly to that. He killed her favorite horse and burned down the castle where they lived with all the staff inside. He told Katie that he would rather kill her than give her a divorce. Both the police in U.K and John MacAulay have been tracking him since," Barbara said.

"I have received information that he entered New Jersey. We have his phone and credit card tracked. As soon as he moves, we will know," John said.

"Katie is obviously very upset and scared at this moment in time. I have vowed to protect her. This meeting is to find out if anyone will support me in that vow and to inform you of the situation," Barbara said.

"How much, does this husband know about Katie's location?" A voice asked.

"Not much. He knows that I live in on a ranch in Houston. He also knows my phone number. That's all," Barbara said.

“Katie had no idea how violent her husband could be. She knew he had a temper; that’s all. The fact remains that she is one of us and I will protect Katie the same way I would any of you,” John said.

“I will protect her, too,” a voice said.

“Me too,” said another.

“Me too,” someone else said.

“Unless anyone objects, I am just going to say she has our full support and you are all in favor of protecting Katie,” John said.

No-one answered.

“That’s settled then,” John said.

Barbara sighed, she was so relieved.

“Thank you, everybody. Really. Thank you from the bottom of my heart,” Barbara said.

"Anytime, I get an update on the husband's movement. I will call a meeting right away. In the meantime, we will just continue as normal. It may just be an empty threat, but it is best to be prepared," John said.

"Thank you for coming, everyone," Barbara said.

The people slowly left, shaking Barbara and John's hand. Barbara was so glad the meeting was over. She had been dreading it all day. She began putting chairs away.

"It's okay. John and I will tidy up. You go on home now," Susie said, giving Barbara a hug.

"Oh, thank you, Susie," Barbara said.

"Bye, John," Barbara said.

"Bye, Barbara! Keep in touch," John said.

"I will," Barbara said.

Barbara left, slowly walked to her car, and drove back home. She was tired now, but she was glad that was over. As

Barbara walked in, Katie was on the sofa, having a pillow fight with Joshua.

"Barbara, your home," Katie said as Joshua hit her on the back of the head with a pillow.

"Yes, I win," Joshua said.

"I was distracted. That doesn't count, Joshua."

"How old are you two? A pillow fight? Really, Joshua?"

"You're in trouble," Katie said.

"Katie! Don't be smug," Barbara said.

"If it's okay, I am going to go, now. Barbara," Joshua said.

"Yes, thank you. I will see you in the morning," Barbara said.

"Bye, Joshua!" Katie said.

"I am tired," Barbara said.

"Oh, sit down. Here's a pillow. I made chicken and salad, I will also make you a cup of tea."

"Thank you, Katie. That was very nice of you."

Barbara sat on the sofa with her feet on the stool, while Katie brought her a plate of food and a cup of tea.

"Katie! I need to tell you something."

"Sounds serious. It's not more bad news, is it?"

"No, Katie, of course not. I think you have been through enough. Today, along with John and Susie MacAulay. I held a town meeting about all this business with Roy."

"Barbara! Why did you do that?"

"The town had a right to know. I mean, what happens if he did turn up and people didn't know?"

"Okay, what happened?"

"The entire town has vowed to protect you from Roy. If the worst happens and he does show up, the whole town will protect you. They want to help because they think of you fondly."

"Barbara! That's great. Thank you really, but I don't want to involve anyone. Too many have died and suffered already. And I know I couldn't have changed that. I really don't want anyone else hurt. Not on my account. Plus, a lot of these people are friends and I would do anything to protect them from this mess."

"Katie! I understand. I truly do, but it's already done. Don't you see that your friends and neighbors feel the same way, about you. They just want to keep you from harm."

"Okay, let's hope he never comes here then."

Katie made herself a cup of tea and sat down next to Barbara before heading upstairs to bed for the night.

She just doesn't understand how dangerous this situation with Roy may get. Katie thought.

Chapter 33

Katie awoke early the following day. She showered and got ready for work.

Time to get back to normal. I can't let Roy get to me.

Katie continued downstairs, where Barbara was making breakfast.

"Morning, Barbara!"

"Morning, Katie! Are you going into work?"

"Yeah, I must be missing Bryan or the horses or something."

Katie sat at the table and starting eating. There was fresh fruit with honey, natural yogurt, toast, jam, and coffee to finish everything off.

"Breakfast is lovely. Thanks."

"You're welcome. Are you sure you are okay?"

"Yes. I am good. It's just time to get back to normal and stop worrying."

"Okay, I just worry; that's all."

"I know Barbara! It's okay. I will see you at lunchtime."

"Bye, Katie!"

As Katie was leaving Joshua walked in and said,

"Oh good. You are back at work. Bryan was missing his partner in crime."

"Morning, Joshua! See you later."

Katie left and made her way down to the stables. The sun was shining brightly in the sky and Katie was glad to get some fresh air.

"Morning, Bryan!"

"Katie, you're here! Great. Alex was starting to drive me crazy."

"Hey! What did I do?" Alex said.

"Morning, Alex!"

"Morning, Katie!"

Katie was happy to be back at work. She was happy to be around the horses again. The three of them worked hard, and it was soon lunchtime. Katie headed back up to the house to see Barbara. When Katie walked in, Joshua was sitting at the table, eating a sandwich.

"Hello, Barbara!"

"Hello, Katie!"

"Is Joshua eating my sandwich?"

"What! No. You think all food is yours," Joshua laughed.

"I am just joking."

"Did you have a good morning Katie?" Barbara asked, bringing her some lemonade.

"Yeah. I love working with the horses."

Katie took a bite of a sandwich and a sip of her drink.

"I was thinking of taking Goliath for a ride when I finish this afternoon," Katie said.

"Great. You want some company?" asked Joshua.

"You can come along if you want as long as you can keep up."

"I'll manage. Meet me at the stables about 5 p.m.."

"You got it."

"Nice to see you two getting on so well," Barbara said.

"Yeah, got to run, see you later."

"Hold on, Katie. I will walk down with you. I need to see Bryan!" Joshua said.

Katie went back to work. The afternoon soon passed, and Katie went back to the house to get changed. Barbara was passed out on the sofa, which she often did when tired or it was too hot. Katie made her way upstairs to get showered and changed. When she was ready Katie went back downstairs, made a cup of tea, and sat at the table until it was time to go meet Joshua at the stables. Katie was really looking forward to going riding. The fact that Joshua was coming too was just a bonus. Katie had missed talking to Joshua. He had been a bit distant for a while, and she was sure she hadn't done anything wrong, but it seemed strange to not talk to him and have a long conversation. She needed him and his advice more than, ever, with everything that was going on. She had to find a way to avoid people here being involved it the mess with Roy and to keep everyone safe. Katie slowly walked toward the stables. Joshua was waiting outside.

"You ready then?" Joshua asked

"Of course," Katie said.

They walked inside the stables. Joshua helped Katie mount Goliath and then went and mounted his horse. They rode out the stables and off the ranch into the countryside. Once they were on a dirt track, they picked up speed going faster and faster. Katie was feeling free and wild, and Joshua was a good rider, so he was able to keep up.

"Let's go into the woods. There's a nice stream there, where the horses can rest," Joshua said.

"Okay, I will follow you," Katie replied.

Katie followed Joshua through the woods and down to the stream. They both dismounted from their horses.

"Good boy, Goliath!" Katie said, leaning forward to pat him as he trotted down towards the stream.

Katie sat on an old tree stump. Joshua sat on the ground next to her.

"You're a really good rider," Katie said.

"Round here we are taught to ride before we can walk," Joshua replied.

"That would explain it."

"So, how are you really doing, Katie."

"How do you think?"

"Honestly! I don't know. I can't imagine, what you're going through. Plus, I've never had a real relationship like the one I have with you."

"Sometimes, I think you're lucky."

"Lucky? Why?"

"Everyone here knows each other. You all know what you mean to each other. I don't think I ever knew Roy."

"I guess, I never thought of it like that."

"So, do you really think he will come here? I heard about the meeting at the town hall."

"I really think he means to kill me! But who knows what he will do? He has lost his mind, which makes him unpredictable."

"You know, you are safe here though. No-one is going to let him hurt you."

"People think they can keep me safe. I don't believe it. If Roy really means to kill me, he will find a way. I am just worried who else will get hurt."

That's it. Roy means to kill me, but if I am somewhere else, no-one will get hurt. Katie thought

"I can understand that Katie! but what will be will be."

"Joshua, what if I was somewhere deserted, no-one would get hurt and if he thinks I am somewhere else he won't come here."

"Where would you go? Where would you tell him you were? What if he found you and you're all alone?"

"I'll tell him I am going home. He won't question that."

"Katie! Please, you must think this through fully. Promise me you will talk this through with Barbara before you do anything."

"Okay Joshua. You worry too much."

"Only because I care. Let's go back, and we can talk to Barbara."

"Okay, we should get the horses back. I could go to Canada."

"Canada?"

"That's where I'll go. There's a family friend that has a lodge in the middle of nowhere, I'll stay there."

"Let's get you back. We will talk all this through. You have to be careful, Katie."

"Yeah, okay."

Katie walked over and remounted Goliath, while Joshua mounted his horse. Katie followed Joshua as they slowly trotted out of the woods and made their way back to the ranch. Katie and Joshua settled the horses in the stables. Joshua took Katie's hand and walked slowly up to the house. Barbara sat at the table doing some paperwork. Katie and Joshua walked up to the table. Joshua held Katie's hand tightly and said,

“Barbara! We need to have a talk with you. It’s important.”

“It’ll wait if you’re busy,” Katie said.

“Oh, no. It won’t wait,” Joshua replied.

“I’m just catching up on paperwork. It is nothing that won’t wait. Take a seat,” Barbara said.

“Katie has something she needs to discuss.”

“Oh, she’s Pregnant!”

“No! I am not pregnant.”

“Just tell her, Katie!” Joshua said.

“Stop being bossy, Joshua!

“I am not bossy!” Joshua replied.

“I have to agree with Katie! You kind of are sometimes.” Barbara said.

“Anyway, I was thinking about the Roy situation. I think and, I found a solution,” Katie said.

“Me, too. Let’s just go to New Jersey and shoot him. We can say it was self-defense,” Barbara said.

“I give up. You two are as bad as each other. Barbara what is wrong with you today?” Joshua replied.

“Sorry, I had a lot of ice cream.”

“Ice-cream?”

“Yeah, I think I have a brain freeze. Continue on Katie.”

“Well, we don’t need to shoot him. But if I am someplace else, no one gets hurt. I’ll go hide in Canada until he’s given up and is out of the United States. We’ll tell him I am going home and, that I came to my senses, as he likes to say.”

“Oh, you know what? That just may work. Here’s what we’ll do. Get the details of where in Canada you are going to, and then we will book a ticket to England from your old account. I will put some money in there. Then I will phone Roy to tell him you’re on the way and to meet you at the airport. Meanwhile, you can go to Canada and hide. Hopefully, once he goes home. That Michael will get a hold of him and talk sense into him. Either that or he'll get arrested for the fire," Barbara said.

"Katie, so you are actually going to do this?" Joshua asked.

"Yes, it's perfect," Katie said.

"And what if he finds you?"

"Then, I'll shoot him."

Joshua sat, shaking his head and said,

"I am coming with you. To keep you safe."

"Oh, Joshua, you don't have to," Katie said.

"Yes, I do."

"It's all settled then. Let's have a drink to celebrate," Barbara said.

"I will make some coffee," Joshua said.

Joshua walked over and started making coffee.

"So, Joshua, who's going to do your job while you're gone?" Katie asked.

"I will talk to, Bryan. He's the only one that's capable," Joshua said.

"I could do it," Barbara said.

"Erm, don't you think it would be a bit much for you?" Joshua asked.

"Yeah, Barbara! I haven't seen you do any work since I arrived. What, is it that you do?"

"Katie, you're so sassy," Barbara replied.

"No, seriously. I am curious!"

"Well, I basically run the office, do the paperwork, sign the cheques, run promotions, that type of thing."

"Okay, do you have an office?"

"Yes, it's a home office that is next to my bedroom."

"Oh! You mean that room filled with boxes?" Katie asked.

"Yes, Katie!"

They all sat and quietly drank their coffee. When they finished. Joshua went home, and Katie sat on the sofa with her feet up and watched some television.

"Don't mind me. I'm just going to finish the paperwork," Barbara said.

"Okay. Let me know if you need anything."

"I will," Barbara said.

Katie turned back around and continued watching television, which she did for most of that night, while Barbara worked on paperwork that she had been neglecting.

Chapter 34

The following morning Katie woke up early. She showered, changed, and then sat down to call her father's friend, Troy. Troy lived in Canada. He owned the lodge that Katie was hoping to go hide in.

"Hello, Troy! It's Katie Maddison, Robert's daughter."

"Hiya, Katie! I remember you. How are you?" Troy said.

"I've been better, to be honest."

"How can I help?"

"I know this is cheeky, but I was wondering if I could use the lodge for a little while. I'll explain. I have this issue with my husband Roy. I left him, and he murdered my horse and burned down our home with people inside. Now is threatening to come kill me. I need to get out of the way for a while," Katie said.

"Oh, really! Sounds like a right kerfuffle. You mean the shack, right?" Troy asked.

"Oh, yeah dad said you called it that. It's huge though. A shack is like a shed."

Troy laughed "It's yours for as long as you want it. I am going to away for a little while but not until next week. Can you get here before then?"

"Yes, thank you. I am going to bring my friend, Joshua, with me. I am staying in Texas now. I will let you know when we will be arriving. Thank you so much. So, you are still in Ontario, right?"

"Yes, in Meaford. Don't worry Katie, you will be safe here."

"Thanks! I'll talk to you soon."

Katie put the phone down and sighed in relief. She went downstairs to make coffee. Barbara was already up.

"Morning, Katie! Coffee is on the table. I am just making toast now."

"Great. It's like you read my mind," Katie said, sitting down at the table.

"Here we go," Barbara said, bringing the toast over.

"Thanks. So, I phoned my dad's friend in Canada this morning," Katie said.

"Oh, what did he say?"

"He says, I can stay at the lodge as long as I need, but I need to get there before next week because he's going away."

"Okay. So, where exactly in Canada is it?" Barbara asked.

"It's in Meaford, Ontario."

"Okay, I will check which airport is nearest to it, and we need to call Joshua to see how soon he can be ready to leave."

"I can hardly believe I am doing this," Katie said.

"It'll all be over soon enough, and then we can get back to normal."

"I am surprised you are not, more nervous about spending all that time alone with Joshua!" Barbara said.

"You know, I'm not sure what it is about Joshua. I always feel completely comfortable around him. It's like feeling at home, like you belong somehow," Katie said.

"Have you ever told him that?" Barbara asked.

"No, I've never really said it."

"Maybe, you should."

"Maybe," Katie said.

Barbara started to clear the table and wash the dishes. Katie got a cloth from the kitchen and wiped down the table, before sitting on the sofa and playing with her mobile phone.

"Are you calling Joshua?" Barbara asked.

"No, I don't have Joshua's number," Katie said.

“Oh, you do not? It’s in my address book just by the side of you.”

Katie looked to the side table. A small, light blue address book was on it. Katie flicked through it until she found Joshua’s number.

“Hey, is Joshua’s last name Garcia?” Katie asked.

“Yes, it didn't he tell you that?”

“No, I’ll call him now,” Katie said.

“Yes, please. Just ask him to come over. I am almost done the cleaning,” Barbara said.

Katie dialed Joshua’s number,

“Hello Joshua answered.

“Hello, Joshua. It’s Katie.”

“Katie, how did you get my number?” Joshua asked.

“Barbara. We need you to come around to discuss Canada,” Katie said.

"Okay, I won't be long."

"See you in a minute," Katie said, before putting the phone down.

Katie turned around to look at Barbara, who was coming out of the kitchen.

"He's coming around," Katie said.

"Good, I think the nearest airport will be Toronto Pearson International Airport. It's around 100 miles from Meaford though so it might be a good idea to hire a car," Barbara said.

"That sounds good."

"The sooner we get this all over with the better."

Joshua walked into the house.

"Hello, Barbara. Hello, Katie," he said.

"Hello, Joshua," They answered together.

"So, Canada!" Joshua said.

"How soon can you be ready to go?" Barbara asked.

"I am ready when Katie is. I need to tell Bryan that I am leaving. I already talked to him about covering my work while I am gone."

"Okay. We can book the tickets today," Barbara said.

"I spoke to my family friend, and it's all set for us to stay there," Katie said.

"Great! Just let me know when you booked the tickets," Joshua said.

"Katie and I need to go into town. We will call later with the details," Barbara said.

"We do?" Katie asked.

"Yes, we need to put the money into your old account to book your ticket to England to fool Roy into going home," Barbara said.

"Oh, yes I had forgotten about that."

"Okay, then. That's everything. You will likely be leaving in the morning, but I will confirm everything later," Barbara said.

"Okay, then. I am going to go and let you two ladies get on with your day," Joshua said.

"Bye, Joshua," Katie and Barbara said together.

"I suppose we should get ready and go into town then," Barbara said.

"I am ready when you are."

"Okay, I am just going to get changed."

Barbara was soon ready, and she and Katie left for town.

"So, do we know how much money to put into the old account?" Katie asked, realizing she had no idea of what things cost.

"Yes. Don't worry. Just give me your bank details, and I will take care of it all," Barbara said.

"Of course. This will work, right?"

"Yes, of course, it will. Are you having second thoughts? Because now would be the time to tell me."

"No. I still think this is the best way to take care of the Roy problem. I am just nervous, I think."

"Okay. We're at the bank," Barbara said.

"Here. My account details are on this bank card," Katie said, handing her the card.

They both walked inside, and Katie moved to the side as Barbara approached the counter.

"How can I help you today?" The bank teller said.

"I need to put some money into this account," Barbara said. She handed the bank teller, the card and money.

The bank teller looked at the card and counted the money and said,

"I can take care of that for you, do you any identification for this account?

Katie passed Barbara her passport which Barbara handed the bank teller. The bank teller checked Katie's passport and handed it back and after she had finished typing said,

"That's all done for you. Is there anything else I can help with?"

"No. Thank you," Barbara said.

"Have a nice day," the bank teller said as Katie and Barbara left the bank.

"That's all done. We will book the plane tickets at home," Barbara said.

Once they were back at the ranch. Katie made some tea, and Barbara got her laptop out to look for plane tickets. Katie brought the tea over and sat down in front of the side table.

"Okay, Katie, so this is my plan. You and Joshua leave for Canada, and then I call Roy once you're gone. I tell him you are arriving in London because you have had a change of heart," Barbara said.

"Okay. Let's look for tickets," Katie said.

"Okay, there are flights to Canada tonight. It takes about 8 hours."

"Okay. Book that. I'll text Troy and Joshua."

"Okay, tell Joshua to be here by 6 p.m.."

"I am going to book you a ticket to London leaving at 6 a.m. tomorrow. It will get to London nine hrs. later."

"That sounds good," Katie said.

Barbara typed away on the laptop, booking the tickets. When she was finished, she said,

"It's all done."

"Thank you. I don't know what I'd do without you."

"You're welcome."

I'll make the most of this time with Barbara.

As Barbara and Katie sat drinking their tea, it occurred to Katie that the next few hours would be the last they would spend together for a while at least. Katie had gotten used to Barbara being there every day.

"Would you help me pack for Canada? I 'm not sure what to take," Katie said.

"Okay, we can do it in a minute if you like," Barbara said.

I am really going to miss Katie while she's gone. I hope she'll be okay!

"Yes, great," Katie said.

Katie and Barbara finished their tea and then went upstairs to Katie's room. Barbara helped Katie to pack a selection of clothes for Canada. They enjoyed this time together. Barbara decided to cook a meal for Katie and Joshua before they left, and Katie decided to go and say goodbye to Goliath while Barbara cooked.

"I'll be back soon," Katie said.

"Okay, no hurry."

Katie took a slow walk down to the stables to see Goliath. She decided to take him to go sit down in a field. It was a sunny day. Katie got Goliath ready and slowly walked him down to the field. She gave him a big hug.

"Goliath, I love you so much. I have to go away for a little while. I need to keep everyone safe from Roy. I won't let him hurt anyone else. I won't let him hurt you. So, I am going to Canada for a little while until this mess is all sorted out. Bryan will take care of you though," Katie said to her horse.

Goliath sat down on the grass, and Katie snuggled into him. They just sat there in silence for a little while.

"Come on, boy. We better get back," Katie said, rising to her feet.

Goliath stood up with her, and they walked back to the stables. Katie settled Goliath in his stall and whispered, "Goodbye Goliath." She walked back to the house.

"Hello, Katie. Dinner will be really soon, and Joshua is on his way over," Barbara said.

"Thank you. It smells lovely."

"Yes, I am doing a Sunday roast with apple pie and ice cream."

"Lovely, I am sure Joshua will love the dessert."

"How was Goliath?"

"He's fine."

Katie got a glass of water. She was starting to feel emotional now that she had started saying goodbyes. Luckily, Joshua soon arrived to distract her with the smallest bag she had ever seen.

"Hello, Barbara. Hello, Katie," he said.

"Hello, Joshua," Barbara said.

"Hello, Joshua. Where are your clothes?" Katie asked.

"They're in here," Joshua answered, pointing at the small bag by his feet.

"Really, are you sure you packed enough?"

"I have everything. No need to worry."

Katie went into the kitchen.

"Can I help with anything?" Katie asked.

"You could set the table for me. Everything is just about done," Barbara said.

Katie began setting the table, and Joshua came over to help her. It was soon all done, so Katie went and got her bag while Barbara put dinner on the table.

The dinner looked and smelled great. They all sat around the table and ate together like a little family. Barbara smiled as she poured some lemonade into glasses. Katie smiled back, taking one of the glasses. After dinner, Barbara dished dessert out mainly, so Joshua wouldn't eat all the apple pie to himself. Everyone was silent. It was almost time to leave. Katie took a deep breath.

"Thank you, Barbara. That was lovely," she said.

"Yes, it was perfect as always," Joshua added.

"Thank you. Well, I suppose we better leave for the airport," Barbara said.

As all three of them walked out of the house, Katie stopped and turned around for one last look around before picking up her bag and closing the door behind her.

Chapter 35

Barbara drove Katie and Joshua straight to the airport.

"Goodbye, Barbara," Katie said.

"Goodbye. Katie, call me when you get there," Barbara said.

"I will, I promise."

"Bye, Barbara," Joshua said.

"Goodbye, Joshua," Barbara said.

Katie and Joshua got their bags, walked into the airport, and checked in for their flight. Barbara headed straight back to the ranch to call Roy.

I really hope this works and they are home safe soon.

It wasn't long before Barbara was back at home. She made a cup of tea and sat on the sofa. She sighed. Katie's flight to England was booked for 6 a.m. the following day. Barbara thought about how much time Roy would need to get back to England. She thought it best to call him immediately.

“Hello, Roy! It’s Barbara,” She said.

“Barbara! What can I do for you?” Roy asked.

“It’s about Katie.”

“Of, course it is. What about her?”

“She’s coming home!”

“What exactly do you mean?”

“Well, she had a change of heart and decided that she wanted to come home. She’s booked on a flight leaving at 6 a.m.,” Barbara said.

“Why isn’t Katie calling?” Roy asked.

“She’s sleeping and she’s a bit worried about how you would take it.”

“What has she told you?”

“Just that you two have had some ups and downs recently,” Barbara said.

"So, what airport is she flying into and what time is she landing?" Roy asked.

"She is coming into Heathrow at 9 a.m. London time."

"Okay, I will meet her."

"Thank you, Roy."

"Take care. Can you make sure Katie calls me once she arrived, so I know she got there safely?" Barbara said.

"Yes, I will. Thank you for calling," Roy said.

I hope he believed that.

Barbara switched on the television and lay down on the sofa relieved.

Meanwhile in New Jersey, in a hotel room, Roy sat at a desk.

So, she thinks she can just come back. I wonder what she's thinking. I mean there's no castle. She has no friends. Maybe she really does love me! Either way, only one way to find out.

Roy opened the laptop that was sat on the desk, he opened it and booked the next flight out of New Jersey to London, which was in a few hours. Then he checked out of the hotel and headed for the airport.

It wasn't long before Roy was on a plane heading for London. He was glad he was going to get there a few hours before Katie arrived, but he was still feeling unsure about what he would do when he finally saw her.

Roy had felt so much pain when Katie had announced she wouldn't come home, and now he just felt numb. There was nothing no joy that she was coming back to him. No pain or hurt either. At least before there were anger and hate. It was intense and out of control, but ever since Barbara's call, that had subsided. Roy no longer knew what it was that he wanted.

If she does love me and I forgive her for the pain she has caused. What would we even do?

Roy's flight landed, and he quickly cleared customs. Roy got a taxi to the nearest hotel, and he booked a room for the night. Roy wanted to shower and change before meeting Katie. He was still unsure about how he felt. Roy had breakfast sent to the room and enjoyed some food while reading the newspaper that was in his room. He was trying to relax and calm himself before heading back out.

Chapter 36

Meanwhile, Barbara was in the house when there was a knock at the door. It was John MacAulay.

"Hello, Barbara. Sorry to stop by unannounced. Can I come in?" John asked.

"Hello, John! Of course. Would you like a cup of coffee?" Barbara asked.

"No, I can't stay long. Is Katie around?"

"No, John. She went to Canada for a few days."

"Okay, well I need to speak to her about that husband of hers. He has left New Jersey and is flying back to London as we speak."

"Oh, that's, great news! Katie will be so happy. I will text her and ask her to call you. She only left tonight so she will still be on her flight," Barbara said.

"That would be great. Have Katie check in with me. I have to go. Bye, Barbara," John said.

"Bye, John," Barbara said, closing the door behind him. Barbara decided to go to bed. She sent a quick text asking Katie to check in with John because Roy was on route to England.

Thank God. Roy seems to have been fooled for now.

Back in London, it was time for Katie's flight to come in. Roy was standing in the arrivals lounge waiting for Katie. He still wasn't completely sure what he was doing, so he just waited there patiently. The arrivals board indicated that Katie's flight had arrived. People were walking through the arrivals lounge now. Roy decided to sit down. Time passed very slowly, but it had been about an hour since the flight had arrived and there was still no sign of Katie. Roy got a feeling of dread in the pit of his stomach.

Maybe she's just stuck in Customs or something.

Roy sat there for another hour. That feeling in his stomach got worse and worse. It turned from dread to tension. He imagined a large ball of tension in the pit of his stomach, just waiting to explode. Roy stood up and walked over to the arrivals desk.

“Hello! I am supposed to be meeting someone arriving from the 6 a.m. Houston to Heathrow flight,” he said as calmly as he could.

“That flight arrived on time, sir if you give me the passenger’s name I could check to see if they boarded,” the desk assistant said.

“Thank you. It’s Mrs. Katie Maddison-Kyle,” Roy said.

The assistant looked on the computer.

“Mrs. Katie Maddison-Kyle was booked on that flight, but she never boarded it. But according to the computer, she boarded a flight from Houston bound for Ontario,” The assistant said.

"She what? Are you sure, it's my wife? I need to be sure where she is!"

"Yes, sir, that's all the information I have. I am sorry."

"Thank you," Roy said. As he turned to walk away, Roy could feel that ball of tension turning to anger. He had so much anger that all that mattered was revenge.

Did they really think they could trick me? I'll show Katie just how wrong she is!

Roy walked to the ticket counter and bought a ticket for the next flight to Canada.

Chapter 37

Katie and Joshua arrived in Ontario. Katie waited outside while Joshua went to rent a car. Joshua appeared with the keys. As they approached the parking lot, Katie quickly realized Joshua had hired a truck. She was shocked to see a beautiful, silver Ram 1500 Crew Cab.

"What's this?" Katie asked.

"It's a pick-up truck," Joshua answered.

"Did they run out of cars?"

"No. Trust me, a car would be suspicious, where we're going."

Katie gave Joshua the driving instructions that Troy sent her, and they drove out of the airport.

"How long did you rent the truck for?" Katie asked.

"A week, but we can return it earlier or extend it if needed," Joshua answered.

"Okay, great."

"I never realized how pretty Canada is! Lucky that, we got to come here."

"Yeah, I guess," Joshua answered.

Katie decided to let Joshua concentrate for a while. It was a long drive, so she took a little nap. Joshua put the radio on very low, so he didn't wake her. It was about an hour later when Katie awoke. Katie looked out of the window. There was a huge lake shimmering in the sunshine. It was, lined with tall evergreen trees for as far as she could see.

It's so beautiful.

"Hey Joshua," Katie said.

"Oh, Katie you're awake. Are you okay?" Joshua asked.

"Yes, I am okay. Thanks."

"So how far have we got to go?"

"We're just over half-way, so it is about forty minutes."

"Great. Do you mind if I turn the radio up?"

"Not at all."

Katie leaned over, turned the radio up, and started singing along. Joshua laughed at her.

"You are full of surprises; do you know that?" Joshua asked.

"Why?"

"I never knew you could sing!"

"I don't really. I only sing along with the radio sometimes," Katie said.

"Your voice is lovely. You should sing more often." Joshua said.

"I'll think about it."

Katie continued singing, and Joshua joined in on a few songs. Soon they were driving down the dusty road that led to the lodge, Joshua pulled the truck up alongside the lodge. The lodge was amazing. It was perched above the treetops. It was a wooden two-story house in a L shape. It was surrounded by woodlands. It had private desks all the way around it.

"This doesn't seem right," Joshua said.

"What? This is Troy's shack, as he calls it. I have only ever seen it in pictures. It's so much more beautiful now I see it for real!" Katie replied.

"That's the lodge?"

"Yes!"

"I thought you said Troy was a redneck?"

"He's not a poor redneck Joshua!"

"Okay, this isn't that I was expecting."

"Oh, there's Troy. Come on," Katie said, jumping out the truck.

A man was walking towards them, He was tall and very muscular. He wore a camouflage T-shirt and jeans with boots. His hair was brown, and he had blue eyes. He was smiling.

"Hello, Troy!" Katie said.

"Katie, good to see you," Troy said, picking Katie up and swinging her around.

"You must be Joshua. Katie said she was bringing a friend. Nice truck by the way," Troy said.

"Thank you, sir," Joshua said, shaking Troy's hand.

"None of that 'sir' stuff. Call me Troy."

"Okay," Joshua replied.

"So, how was your trip?" Troy asked.

"It was good. Long but good," Katie said.

"Great! Well, I have made some food. Let's go inside," Troy said.

Joshua followed Katie and Troy inside. They walked into the living room. There were a cork floor and two floral sofas.

Troy's prize baseball bat hung on wall, and there was a large deer head above the fire. Behind one of the sofas, there was a dining table and four chairs made from oak with floral cushions on them. There was lots of food on the table. There was, fried chicken and onions rings, bread, butter, fries, salad, homemade salsa, and an apple pie.

As they sat at the table, Katie asked.

"Did you do all this, Troy?"

"No, my wife Josie did. She will join us in a minute," Troy said.

Just then a woman walked in. She was tall and had long dark hair. She was tan and wore shorts and a camouflage t-shirt. She had a kind smile, and her brown eyes sparkled.

"Hello. I am Josie," she said.

"Hello, Josie! Nice to meet you," Katie said.

"Hi, Josie!" Joshua said.

“Hey, baby!” Troy said.

“Hey, babe! you want does anyone want a cold drink?”

“Can I have a cola, please?” Katie asked.

“Babes get me and Joshua a beer. You do drink beer, Joshua?” Troy asked.

“Yeah, beer is fine,” Joshua said

“Be right back,” said Josie.

Josie came back with three beers, and a glass of cola for Katie and set them down on the table. They ate lunch. Katie loved fried chicken, and she took some pie before Joshua ate it all. After dinner, Katie went out on the deck to call Barbara. As Katie finished talking to Barbara, Troy came out and stood next to Katie on the deck.

“So, are you going to tell me about this Roy guy?” Troy asked.

“Okay, Troy,” Katie replied.

Katie explained about Roy and everything that had happened.

"You should have called when he hit you, Katie," Troy said.

"I know, anyway, he's in New Jersey or I have tricked him into thinking I was going back so he went back to meet me. I am hoping he stays there," Katie said.

"Is the divorce, so you can marry Joshua?" Troy asked.

"What? No, Joshua's just a friend. I mean I like him, of course, I do," Katie said glancing through the glass door behind them.

"I had to ask. He seems like a good guy," Troy laughed.

"Yeah, he is. Josie seems nice, too," Katie said.

"She's great. God knows why she puts up with me though!"

"We are going to stay here the night. Then we are going to leave tomorrow to visit friends in Vermillion. If you need me, just call. You'll be safe here. The local police and hospital details are on the inside of the kitchen cupboard," Troy said.

"Thank you, Troy. Really thanks for everything. I can't believe how beautiful it is here."

"Yeah, it's nice enough."

"Joshua was eating pie, last I saw," Troy said.

"Yeah, that boy really loves pie."

"Katie! Does your dad know, about Roy and everything that he has done?" Troy asked.

"No, I haven't seen my family for years. Roy kept me away from everyone," Katie said, as she turned away.

"Easier to control that way, no doubt! You should call your dad sometime, Katie," Troy said

"I will when this is all over and it's safe."

Katie continued inside and walked up to Joshua, who had just finished the pie.

"Want to go for walk, Joshua?" Katie asked.

"Yeah, sure!" Joshua replied.

"See you in a while, Josie!" Katie said.

"Bye, Josie! Bye Troy!" Joshua said.

Katie and Joshua walked outside and headed towards the woods.

"They seem like nice people," Joshua said.

"Yeah, I mean, Troy's great. That's the first time. I've met Josie."

"So, where are we going?"

"I thought we could just walk and explore."

"Okay, then."

Joshua took Katie's hand in his hand, and they walked down through the trees into the woods. The sun was shining through the trees. Katie could hear the birds singing.

"It's nice to just walk and not be rushing about, isn't it?" she said to Joshua.

"Yes, it is nice spending time with you, knowing no-one's watching!" Joshua replied.

"Yeah! you have been distant lately."

"I guess, we were getting close."

"Yeah! Does getting close to me scare you?

"It's a funny feeling. I am not scared exactly," Joshua answered.

"Can you explain it?"

There was a sound of water cascading near-by.

"Can I hear water?"

"Yes, I think it's this way. Come on."

Katie and Joshua made their way through the trees to their right. Where the tree's cleared, there was a ravine with a winding rock path leading down to it. They suddenly realized they stood at the top of a cliff face. The cliff face was steep and form a v-shaped platform over the ravine below.

"That's amazing," Katie said.

"It really is. Don't get too close to the edge."

"You're so protective."

"Well, I am here to keep you safe."

"That's very true."

Katie and Joshua took a slow walk back to the lodge. Joshua stopped outside on the deck.

"Joshua, what's wrong?" Katie asked.

"Nothing, I just want to stand here a little while. Do you mind?" he asked.

"No, we can do anything you want."

"Thank you, Katie."

When they eventually went inside, Katie and Josie sat on the sofa. Troy wanted to show Joshua the gun room. Troy led Joshua down the passage to a door. At the bottom, it had a keypad on it. Troy punched in the code which, he told Joshua was '6739'. The door opened to a small room filled with shelves and a large gun rack in the middle of the wall. It held rifles and shot guns. The shelving housed the bullets, belts, and other accessories. There was gun license framed and hung on the back of the door. There were some fishing rods and fishing equipment by the door.

"Do you shoot, boy?" Troy asked.

"Erm, yes, well my dad taught me to shoot with a '22' rifle, but I don't get much time. I am busy managing the ranch; it, takes a lot of my time!" Joshua replied.

"Ever been shooting with Katie?"

"Katie! No, we...err, go horse riding."

“You should! Katie is good. I taught her myself back in England one time,” Troy said.

“Katie can shoot with one of those?”

“Like a sniper, she’s really good.”

“She never told me that,” Joshua said.

“It was a long time ago, I guess. There’s a pistol in the side Drawer upstairs. It’s Josie’s, you may want to keep it on you just in case.”

“Okay. Thanks.”

Joshua and Troy left the gun room and re-joined the girls in the living room.

“Everything okay?” Katie asked.

“Yeah. Think I freaked your boyfriend out a bit,” Troy laughed.

“Troy!” Katie said.

“Don’t worry. He’ll be fine. Won’t you, Josh?” Troy asked.

"I'm fine, and we're just friends," Joshua said.

"Whatever you say, man," Troy said, as he sat down.

Joshua sat down laughing and shaking his head.

Joshua and Katie sat and had a drink with Troy and Josie before heading up to separate bedrooms for the evening. They were tired from the long flight.

Chapter 38

The following morning, Katie and Joshua were up early. They showered, dressed and headed down- stairs where Josie was making breakfast. Katie could smell the homemade bread.

"Something smells amazing. Josie," Katie said.

"Morning, Katie! That's the bread. I made lots of food. I wasn't sure what you would want," Josie said.

"Thank you; that's very kind. Is Troy still sleeping?"

"Morning, Joshua! Troy is loading up the truck. We are leaving early," Josie said.

"Oh, yeah! Troy did mention it yesterday," Katie replied.

Troy walked in and they all sat down to eat breakfast together.

I wish I could spend more time with Josie and Troy. She seems nice.

"Remember, Katie, we are only going to Vermillion. If you need me, just call," Troy said.

"Thank you, Troy. I am sure we will be just fine," Katie replied.

"See you soon, Katie," Josie said.

"Bye, Josie! Bye, Troy!"

"Bye, Joshua! Bye, Katie!" Josie and Troy said.

Josie and Troy got into their truck and drove off leaving Katie and Joshua by themselves.

"I just thought of something!" Katie said.

"Oh, what's that?" asked Joshua.

"This is the first time we have ever really been alone together."

"Does that bother you, Katie?"

"Not, really!" It does make me a little nervous," Katie said.

"Me, too. But, really it's no different than when we go for horse rides or sit by the river at home."

"I guess you're right. Do you want to go sit by the ravine?"

"Sounds good."

Katie and Joshua put on their boots and starting walking down through the woods towards the ravine.

"It really is peaceful here," Katie said.

"Yeah. Look! There's a path down to the ravine, I wonder how we missed that yesterday," Joshua said.

"No idea. Let's go down there and have a look."

"Okay! Be careful, Katie."

Katie and Joshua careful walked down the path. About halfway down Katie said,

"Look how steep the cliff is from here."

"That's quite a drop," Joshua replied.

They continued down. There were jagged cliffs on one side and a valley off very tall green trees on the other with only the ravine to separate the two sides. Eventually, they reached the bottom. There was a small, narrow gravel path alongside the ravine.

“That water looks fast,” Katie said.

“It does. Stay on the path, Katie.”

“I know. I am not a child.”

“I noticed.”

Katie and Joshua walked around the path, and, to their surprise, it led, back into the woods again. They continued back to the lodge. Katie made a cup of tea and they sat down.

“We should check if there’s anything we need later,” Joshua said.

“Good idea. I will drink this, and then I should call Barbara,” Katie replied.

"Yeah. I want to check on Bryan to make sure he's coping."

"I'm sure he's fine."

Katie and Joshua drank their tea, and Katie went outside to call Barbara while Joshua went into the kitchen to call Bryan.

Katie walked back inside. Joshua was sitting on the sofa again.

"Everything okay?" he asked.

"Yes, great. Barbara says that, Bryan is doing well."

"Yeah, I just spoke to him."

"Good. I had a thought," Katie said.

"Go on, what is it," Joshua asked.

"Well, how will we know when it's safe to go back? I mean, I like it here, but I don't want to stay forever. I never really thought it through."

"I guess we stay the week. If nothing happens and if Barbara doesn't hear anything, we go home. I think it would be a good idea to check the news in England, you know, in case he gets arrested."

"That sounds like a great plan. I can see why Barbara made you manager," Katie said.

"Thank you!" Joshua replied.

"I checked the cupboards. They look well stocked. I don't think we need to worry about food," Joshua said.

"Let's explore the house. I mean we have it to ourselves for a while," Katie said.

"Great idea. Follow me."

Joshua led Katie down the same passage that Troy had taken him the day before to the gun room.

"Now the code is 6739," Joshua said, typing it in on the keypad. Joshua opened the door and he and Katie stepped inside the gun room.

"Wow, this is amazing," Katie said, taking one of the rifles off the wall and holding it.

"So, what's this about you being able to shoot?"

"Well, Troy is my dad's friend. My dad likes hunting. So, Troy taught me years ago. Is that what he said yesterday to freak you out?"

"Well, yes, but it didn't freak me out, I was just surprised."

"Let's go see the rest of the house. You want to go fishing tomorrow? I could ask Troy where the best place is to go, Katie said.

"That sounds great," Joshua said, as Katie put the gun down and shut the door behind them.

Katie and Joshua headed upstairs next. The bathroom which was had white-tiled walls, a bath, a corner shower, a sink and a toilet. Then there were four bedrooms. The first one was where Joshua had slept, and he had left it messy, so he said,

"I slept in there. Nothing to see really."

"Really?" asked Katie, opening the door, a shocked expression slowly spread across her face as she looked around the room.

Inside the room, there was a bed covered in clothes, and it hadn't been made. There were books just thrown on the floor with shorts, a t-shirt, and a dressing gown draped over the chest of drawers.

"You have only been in there one night!" Katie said.

"What? I'm a bit messy," Joshua replied.

"That's like saying Barbara's a bit social! Well, I know what you're doing this afternoon!"

"Okay, I will tidy it up a bit."

"A bit? Come let me show you what a room should look like," Katie said, taking Joshua's hand.

Katie opened the door to the room, she had stayed in. It was perfectly neat. The bed had been made and the pillows plumped. Her nightie was neatly folded and placed at the foot of the bed. Her toiletries bag was tidily placed on the dressing table. The window was slightly open to let fresh air in.

“See, what I mean!” Katie said.

“Okay, I get the point,” Joshua said.

“Let’s go back down-stairs,” Katie said.

“Okay.”

Joshua followed Katie downstairs and Katie got a drink and sat on the sofa.

“If you clean that room, I could cook dinner, and we could sit out on the deck this evening, if you like,” Katie said.

“Okay, I will just have a drink, and then I will get started,” Joshua replied.

Joshua finished his drink and went upstairs.

Later that day, Joshua and Katie were sitting out on the deck, having a drink.

"So, I spoke to Troy earlier. He sent me the details of where to go fishing. Do you still want to go?" Katie asked.

"Yes, I think it will be fun, and we might as well while we are here!" Joshua answered.

"Okay. Then we will need to leave early though."

"Of, course."

The sun was setting over the trees. Katie and Joshua sat and watched. He took her hand and smiled.

After a while, they went back inside, and Katie sat on the sofa and read, Joshua just sat there not sure what to do.

This is strange. All I ever do is work, so I have no idea what to do with myself with all this spare time. Katie looks so absorbed in that book. I love it when she smiles.

Katie and Joshua had an early night that night, so they could be up early to go fishing.

Chapter 39

The following morning, Katie was up and dressed before Joshua was. She was in the kitchen making food for their fishing trip. Katie had already loaded up the truck.

"Good morning, Katie," Joshua said, as he walked into the kitchen.

"Good morning, sleepy head!" Katie said.

"Yeah, I slept well last night. I don't even know how you got all this done without waking me."

"You were snoring your head off when I came downstairs earlier," Katie said.

"Are those peanut-butter and jelly sandwiches?" Joshua asked.

"Yes, and they are for the trip. If you are hungry there's bacon sandwich behind, you!"

"Great. Thank you."

"Pass me that bag, will you? I am about done!"

Joshua reached down and passed Katie the bag from a shelf under the counter.

"Thank you. I will just put this in the truck and then I'm ready when you are."

"I am always ready!" Joshua said, biting into the sandwich as tomato ketchup oozed out and covered his mouth.

"Yes, you look ready, standing there with your mouth covered ketchup," Katie laughed, walking out towards the door.

Joshua wiped his hands, grabbed his jacket and followed her. Katie turned around and Joshua kissed her.

"Now, you're covered in ketchup too," he said.

"Yeah, thanks for that!" Katie said wiping her mouth with some tissue she had in her pocket. Katie walked back towards the lodge and locked it up, then returned to the truck and got in the passenger seat.

"Do you want me to pour you some coffee before we set off?" Katie asked.

"Yes, please. I need the information from Troy to program the GPS too please," Joshua said.

"Okay."

Katie carefully poured a cup of coffee from the flask and handed it to Joshua, before taking out her phone find the text from Troy. She passed it to Joshua.

A few minutes later, they were ready to go. It was about one-hour drive to the place where they were going fishing. Katie took herself a bacon roll out of the bag and put the radio on.

When they arrived at the river the sun had come out and was shining on the water. There were a few others fishing along the riverbank. Joshua started emptying the truck and setting up on a quiet spot on the riverbank. Katie sat on the grassy bank, baiting her fishing rod with spiders.

“Katie, what are you doing?” Joshua asked.

“What does it look like, I am doing!”

“Well, you will never catch anything that way.”

“You see, I thought that the first time too! But this way is so much better.”

“I bet you it won’t work,” Joshua laughed.

“Okay. Whoever catches the first fish, can buy take away on the way back,” Katie said.

“Take away? You mean you’re not, even going to eat the fish you catch?”

“Eww, of course not. I throw them back in. I don’t eat fish!”

“Why, did you suggest coming then?” Joshua asked, he was getting more confused by the moment.

"I love fishing, it's relaxing. My dad used to take me when I was little. He would fish and I would talk about my new shiny shoes. I always had new shiny shoes when I was little," Katie said.

"Have you ever eaten fish?"

"Well, my Auntie Claudiatried to feed me cod once, but she left the room and I starting choking. I never ate fish again. Wait prawns don't count right?"

"That explains a lot! No, prawns don't count," Joshua said.

"Great! I love surf and turf," Katie said.

"Isn't that lobster?"

"Not in England. It's steak and usually battered or pastry coated prawns!"

Katie stood up and threw her line into the water. Joshua soon threw his line in too.

It turned out Katie was right, and it wasn't long before Katie's line was tugging.

"Joshua, can you help me, please?"

Joshua put his rod down and walked behind Katie to help. Joshua slowly slid his arms around her waist and helped her hold the rod, while Katie reels the fish in slowly. Katie froze. She had butterflies in the pit of her stomach. Joshua's arms around her felt so good. Joshua dropped his arms, and Katie was holding a small trout.

"Take a photo so I can throw it back in," Katie said.

Joshua took out his phone and quickly took a photo of Katie and her fish. Katie quickly threw the fish back in the river.

"God, I love you. You're so cute!" Joshua said, before he realized what he was saying.

"Really!" Katie replied.

Not as cute as you, in those jeans!

“Guess, I am buying supper then!” Joshua said.

“That’s the worst attempt to change the subject, I ever saw!” Katie said.

“I was just stating the obvious!”

“About supper? I would rather talk about you thinking I am cute!” Katie said.

“You are not going to let that go? Are you?”

“No way!” Katie said sitting down and passing Joshua a sandwich.”

Joshua was eating slowly, so Katie decided to have lunch too. When they were finished, Katie moved closer to Joshua.

“So, you love me now! Took you long enough,” Katie teased.

“Well, erm, hold on! What do you mean took me long enough?” Joshua asked.

Katie sighed. “Can you just be kissing now please?”

“Yeah.”

Joshua leaned into kiss Katie. He put one hand on her waist and the other hand on the ground. Katie felt herself lean back slightly the kiss was intense and lingering, Katie was losing her balance; she was lost in the kiss. Joshua slowly gently brought the kiss to an end and sat up straight with his hand still on Katie's waist as she opened her eyes, Joshua said.

"I love you!"

"I Love you, Joshua!" Katie said.

"Come on, let's go, Katie!" Joshua said.

"Okay, then."

Katie and Joshua were soon all packed up and back on the road home.

"Hey, Joshua! How about going to a restaurant tonight instead of takeaway? Troy told me about this place in town we could try!"

"Sounds, great."

Once they got back to the ranch and had put the things away, Katie went up for a bath and to get ready to go to the restaurant.

It was about an hour later when Katie came down-stairs and approached Joshua in the kitchen, where he was making a drink.

Joshua saw Katie coming towards him.

Wow. She is so worth the wait. She takes my breath away every time.

Katie was wearing a black cotton shift dress with black high heels. Her hair was up in a messy bun. She looked completely flawless. As she got closer, Joshua realized she smell as good as she looked.

"Hey, Joshua! Everything okay?" Katie asked.

"Yeah, great!" Joshua replied.

"Are you ready to go to dinner?"

"Yes. You look amazing by the way."

"Thank you. You look good too."

They were soon at the restaurant. They walked inside. The restaurant had cream walls with dark wooden trimming. There were plants scattered around the restaurant and artwork on the walls above each table. There were some screens at the end of some tables. The tables and chairs were made of mahogony wood. Katie and Joshua were seated at the far end of the restaurant. Katie was browsing at the menu when the waitress approached.

"Can I get you a drink?" the waitress asked.

"Can I have an orange juice? Katie?" Joshua replied.

"I'll have a glass of wine. White please," Katie said.

"Okay, Then I will be right back with your drinks," the waitress said, as she walked away.

"Orange juice?"

"Yes, it's good for you. I just wanted some, Katie."

"Okay, it was just unusual. That's all."

"Do you know what you want to eat?" Joshua asked.

"I'm not sure yet. What are you having and please don't say steak!"

Joshua laughed. "I am not sure yet."

The waitress approached with the drinks,

"Do you want to order food, or should I come back in few minutes?" she asked.

"I've decided!" Katie said.

"Me, too!"

"Can I have the shrimp fettuccini, please?" Katie said.

"And I will have the New York strip, please," Joshua said.

"Okay, then enjoy your drinks, if you need anything just call me," the waitress said.

"The New York strip has sprouts in it! Do you like eat sprouts?" Katie asked.

"Oh, I love them. I usually only get them at Christmas."

"I am learning, a lot about you today!"

"I guess," Joshua said, turning around and looking around the restaurant.

"This place is nice," Joshua continued.

The food soon arrived. It looked amazing. Joshua's New York strip was a plate of roasted potatoes with spinach, brussels sprouts, with bacon and caramelized onions. They were quiet while they ate their dinner. Katie sipped her wine.

"Is that nice?" Katie asked.

"Yes, it's delicious. How was your dinner?"

"Lovely. Thank you."

After they finished their meal, Katie and Joshua returned to the lodge. Katie made coffee and joined Joshua out on the deck. She handed Joshua a cup of coffee.

"Thank you, Katie."

"It's okay. I was thinking about something. Well wondering really."

"About what, exactly?"

"Well, you said you loved me twice today. You have never said it before, I wondered why."

"Well, okay, truth be told. I have been mesmerized by you since we first met. But you were married and on holiday then. I knew it wasn't right. I am not the kind of guy who breaks-up happy homes, Katie. Sometimes you can be so annoying. You get right under my skin, and other times you're so cute and sweet that, I just want to hold you and not let go. I tried to keep my distance and not let my feelings run away with me at first. It didn't take long to realize I couldn't.

I am crazy about you, and there's no denying or hiding that. To say it out loud would just make it so real and final. I am always going to be here for you because, I am incapable of anything else."

"Thank you, for being so honest. The day I met you, Barbara and I talked about how cute you are in those jeans," Katie laughed. "But I felt the same as you at first, I thought it was wrong and I should try and fight it. If I am honest with myself, I am crazy about you. I never felt like this before, so I am not sure what I am doing. I think about you constantly and there's nothing I wouldn't do for one more kiss in any given moment. It feels so amazing when you put your arms around me. I just what to stay there forever."

"I'd love to just be together, with everything out in the open. We both know, I am not good enough for you! Katie. Look at you, you're stunning," Joshua said, leaning backward and sipping his coffee.

"Joshua, oh Joshua! I never want to hear anything like that come out of your mouth again. Why do you always feel like you need to prove something? You are amazing, and you're always right about everything! You are everything I could ever want and then so much more. All I need is for you to say you love me and always will. I couldn't want you anymore than I already do!"

"You know, I love you. That's the third time in one day, I've said it! I couldn't ever feel any other way about you, Katie."

"Then, let's just be together. I love you, and you're my best friend these days. I just want to be with you forever!" Katie said.

"You know, you're right, let's do it!"

Katie leaned backwards and put her head on Joshua's shoulder. They sat there and watched the sunset before going back inside.

Katie woke up the following morning with a smile on her face. The sun was bursting through the window, and she could hear Joshua, snoring down the hall. Katie got ready and went downstairs. The kettle must have woken up Joshua because he was downstairs before it had even boiled.

"Can I have a cup of coffee?" Joshua asked.

"Morning, Joshua! Yeah, sure," Katie replied.

She sat at the table taking the coffee with her.

"I was thinking we could go to the park, today. We might as well explore Meaford, while we are here!" Katie said.

"Sure. Whatever you want," Joshua replied.

"Are you okay?"

"Yeah, I just need coffee. Lots of coffee!"

"All right!"

A little while later after several cups of coffee, Katie and Joshua were in the truck heading for the park. They soon arrived. Katie took a deep breath. The park was huge. They walked in and found a group of benches nestled under some large trees. It was lovely and shady.

"Joshua," Katie said.

"Yes, Katie!" Joshua replied.

"Well, when are we going home? We have been here a few days now, and nothing has happened here or in Texas. There's nothing in the English news about Roy either, so maybe he has given up."

"Okay. I'll call Barbara tomorrow, if things are still quiet. We can book flights and go home!" Joshua said.

"Great! I miss Barbara and Texas and Goliath. I can't wait to go riding again."

"I know what you mean. It's beautiful here but it's not home!"

Katie and Joshua decided to go explore the park. They walked hand in hand through the open space with a path, green trees and play areas until they came to what looked like a beach. It was right at the back of the park and spread out like it was endless. There was what looked like a little marina with small sailing boats in and around it. The water was perfectly still and crystal blue. Katie and Joshua walked down and found a spot on the sand to sit on.

“I never knew there was a beach here too!” Katie said.

“I think it’s a lake,” Joshua replied.

“That would make more sense, but I’ve seen smaller beaches. At what point does a lake become the sea?”

“You know, I am not sure,” Joshua said.

“What? You mean there’s something you don’t know?” Katie asked.

“Very funny, Katie!”

“It’s beautiful, either way.”

“Yeah, it is.”

Katie lay down on the beach, and Joshua turned to face her.

“It’s nice to just relax, isn’t it?” he said.

“Yes. It is a lovely day, it’s nice to be able to enjoy it.

Later, Katie and Joshua sat on the sofa. They drank the lemonade that Katie had made. Katie got a text message from Troy. It read:

“Hope you’re enjoying yourself; we will be back tomorrow evening. See you both then.”

Katie texted back: “Okay!”

She cuddled back into Joshua on the sofa.

“So, when we go home, are we going to date?” Katie asked.

“Do you want to? Joshua asked back.

"Might be nice. I just want you I don't care about anything else."

Suddenly, Katie phone rang.

"Katie! Finally! I have been trying all day," Barbara said.

"Barbara, what's wrong? Are you okay?" Katie asked.

"It's Roy! Katie."

"What about him? What's he done?"

"He's in Ontario. John called this morning. He's staying at a hotel near the airport," Barbara said.

"Oh God. Does he know where I am?"

"I don't know. But you need to be very careful!"

"Okay, well, we are in the lodge. Don't worry. I will keep in touch. I am going to go to talk to Joshua."

"Bye, Katie!"

"Bye, Barbara!"

Katie put the phone down. The fear showed on her facial expression.

"He's here, isn't he?" Joshua asked.

"He's in Ontario, staying near the airport," Katie replied.

Joshua put his arm around her.

"I won't let him hurt you, Katie!"

"I'm just scared, Joshua!"

"He's what we're going to do. I will lock the doors, and we will get a gun out the gun room. We are ready for him, and it will soon be over with."

"I hope you're right. I need to call Troy. He can't come back to this!" Katie said.

Joshua locked all the doors and checked the lodge.

"Troy! Hi, it's Katie. I have a problem!"

"Katie, what's wrong?" Troy asked.

"The police tracked Roy to a hotel near Ontario airport. I think it's best you stay where you are until it's over," Katie replied.

"Like Hell! I will. I will be back tomorrow. I will leave Josie here."

"Is there any point in arguing?"

"No! Katie, I will see you tomorrow, and make sure you keep the rifle near!"

"Okay, Troy."

"Bye, Katie!"

"Bye, Troy!"

Joshua brought Katie a rifle.

"We are all locked up!"

"Thank you. Troy said, he is coming anyway but alone."

"Maybe that's just as well."

Katie sat back on the sofa. Joshua watched over Katie all night.

Chapter 40

Roy rented a room in a hotel near the airport and hired a car to get him around. Roy was in his hotel room, pacing,

Where would she go? Who does she know in Canada? Why Ontario? What am I missing?

Roy's phone rang.

"Hello, Roy!" Michael said.

"Michael! I am a little busy," Roy replied.

"Yet, you answered your phone finally! I am worried about you. Where are you?"

"I'm safe. I am out of town."

"Well now, I know that much. So, let's try again! I followed you to London and then to New Jersey. Where are you now?"

"Why? Are you stalking me, Michael?" Roy asked.

"I am concerned. So, are you coming home?" Michael asked.

"Not Yet! I have something to do first."

"First? So, you are coming home then?"

"Soon! I will be home soon."

"Okay. Can I help with anything?" Michael asked.

"Depends, are you in touch with Anna?"

"Yes, I am. She has been pumping Katie for information for me. Why?"

"Ask her who Katie knows in Ontario," Roy said.

"Ontario? I thought Katie was in Texas?" Michael asked.

"No, she's in Ontario! I need to see her to confirm the legal grounds on which to divorce her. "

"You are going to divorce her?"

"What else is there to do, Michael!"

"Okay, Roy. I will call you straight back," Michael said, before hanging up.

Roy sat down at the pine desk in his hotel room, feeling contented.

Anna will surely provide the answers I need.

While Roy was feeling smug, Michael dialed Anna's number.

“Anna! How are you?” Michael asked.

“Michael! How are you? Did you find him yet?” Anna asked.

“Not yet, I spoke to him on the phone though. He’s in Ontario. I think he’s stalking Katie! Does she have any connections there? I need to find her before Roy does!”

“Yes, Katie has a family friend there. His name is Troy, she used to talk about him.”

“Troy? Is he just a family friend? Do you know where about in Ontario he lives?”

“Meaford! I will send you a picture of his cabin. If she is there that's where she will be. But before, I send the picture.

You must swear not to share this with Roy! I can trust you, Michael. Can't I?"

"Anna, I am surprised you have to ask. I just need to make sure he doesn't cause any more damage. Hasn't everyone suffered enough?"

"Okay, Michael. Keep me informed!" Anna said.

"Bye, Anna. See you soon," Michael replied.

"Anna hung up and sent Michael the picture of Troy's cabin. She took a deep breath as she hit send on her phone.

Michael called Roy as soon as he had the picture.

"Hello, Michael!" Roy said.

"I spoke to Anna! If Katie's in Ontario. She is in Meaford with a family friend called Troy!" Michael said.

"Michael, you're brilliant."

"You're not going to do anything stupid, are you?"

“No, I am just going to sort grounds for the divorce. Then we can all move on.”

“In that case, I have a photo for you. I will send it now,” Michael said, before sending the photo of the cabin through to Roy.”

Roy received it. “It's a cabin,” Roy said.

“Yes, Roy. It's Troy's cabin. Katie gave that photo to Anna,”

“Great!”

“Stay in touch. Call if you need anything,” Michael said.

“I will. Thanks, Michael! I will see you soon,” Roy replied before hanging up.

Roy grabbed the car keys sitting on the hotel desk and his jacket. He headed for the car. Roy programmed the car’s navigation system for Meaford and started driving. With his mobile on the seat next to him. He was not altogether sure what he would do once he got there.

Should I kidnap her or just kill her? What to do with this family friend? He would have to be gotten out the way before I get my hands on, Katie! She would surely know this area well, and I don't. I am not used to thinking things through! The horse and the fire had been instant like an automatic reaction. I will spy on her a bit. Yes, I will find the lodge and then stalk it out for a few days that will give me time to work out what I am going to do!

Roy arrived in Meaford. He parked the car and walked into a small café. Roy sat down, and a waitress approached the table. She was tall and slim with her brown hair tied back. She was dressed in black with a light green apron,

"Can I get you something?" she asked.

"Oh, yes, can I have a latte, please?" Roy said.

"I'll be back in a minute," she said, turning around and slowly walking away.

Roy watched the rhythm of her legs as she walked away.

Nice!

The waitress soon returned with the latte.

“Thank you,” said Roy.

“If there is anything else you want, let me know,” she said.

“Oh, maybe you could help me. I am visiting my friend. He gave me this photo of the house,” Roy said, showing her the picture.

“Oh, yeah that’s Troy’s place. It’s just off the main road. You follow the main road, and you will come to a turning point just before the woods,” she said.

“Thank you, so much. You have been very helpful.”

Roy drank his coffee, left the café and starting to drive again. It wasn’t long at all before Roy was at the lodge cabin. He continued to drive and drove through the woods to find somewhere to park the car out of sight.

Roy parked the car and walked through the woods until he could clearly see the lodge through gaps in the trees. He saw Katie sitting on the deck outside the lodge.

There you are! Enjoy yourself while you can Katie.

Then Roy saw Joshua join her.

I thought he was her family friend. He seems a bit young!

Roy watched them for a while. He saw Joshua look at Katie and say something. He also saw the way Katie looked at him back. It was like a knife in his chest twisting and turning that was unable break free.

That's not a family friend. I know that look. I remember when she looked at me that way back when we were happy. So, this was it. Katie had fallen for someone else. She lied to me. Well, I will make her pay, her and him as well. I will make Katie watch, while I destroy him. Then it will be her turn. Yes, I will break her heart, and then she will beg me to kill her before I do.

After Katie and Joshua had gone back inside, Roy went back to his car and returned to his hotel room. Roy brought a bottle of whiskey on the way to his room. He went inside and threw the keys on the bed. He poured a glass of whiskey and sat at the desk. The knot in Roy's stomach was back again, the same one he had felt the day of the fire. The rage swelled inside of him. He had to kill Katie. It was the only way to calm the storm inside him. He drank the whiskey, trying to numb the rage inside him. He drank himself to sleep before he numbed the rage.

It was mid-morning when Roy awoke with a headache like tornado swirling round in his head.

Maybe the whiskey wasn't the best idea!

He showered and changed before heading out to get some food. Roy ate in the hotel before getting in the car and driving back out to the lodge. The lodge was empty, and the truck was gone. Roy stayed for a few hours until he saw Joshua and Katie return. Roy noticed that Joshua left the truck door unlocked, and that the only time Katie left his side was if Joshua came out the lodge to get something from the truck.

That's the key. I will get him when he comes out to the truck and let Katie come find him. Then I will punish her, too!

Roy watched the lodge for a while longer. He checked where all the exits to the lodge were, just in case he had to go in there and get Katie.

Tomorrow is the day I will do it. I will get some rest tonight and come early in the morning.

Chapter 41

The following morning. Roy made his way back to Meaford. He did a little shopping first. He stopped to buy a rope, a compass, a hunting knife, and a rifle before heading for the cabin once more. Roy still wasn't sure how or what he was going to do! When he thought of Katie, an uncontrollable rage took over. It had to be satisfied, and the only way to do that was with violence.

I will deal with him first. Roy tucked the hunting knife into his sock. He picked up the rifle and walked to Joshua's truck, he slid the rifle underneath the truck. He then slithered himself under the truck like a snake, on the driver's side and waited for Joshua to come out.

Katie and Joshua were awake inside the house. Katie had made food while Joshua had checked that the house was still secure. They sat at the table now eating bacon sandwiches with coffee.

"How are you doing today, Katie?" Joshua asked.

"I'm okay. I really thought he was going to attack us in the night," Katie said.

"We are perfectly safe in here, and Troy is coming back. It will soon all be over. Once Roy surfaces, we can get him arrested," Joshua said.

I am not sure even I believe this is going to be that easy. Joshua thought.

"Yes, and we can go home. I miss Barbara," Katie said.

"Me too, actually. It's strange not seeing her every day!" Joshua said.

"I should call her."

"Yeah, you do that. I just need to go get my mobile out in the truck. Be back in a minute."

"Joshua, be careful and lock the door behind you."

"Katie, I am only going to the truck!"

Katie sat down with her phone on the sofa. Joshua walked out the door, carefully locking the door behind him. Joshua walked around the truck to the driver's side. He didn't see Roy, who was still hiding just underneath the truck, but now holding the hunting knife. As Joshua reached for the driver's door, he felt a sudden, sharp, stabbing pain in the back of his calf. He looked down to see blood running down to his boots. Roy slid out, and quickly pulled Joshua to the ground and pinned him to the floor with his arm.

"Ouch! Let me guess it's Roy!" Joshua said, tipping his head back and trying to wriggle free.

Roy quickly gagged Joshua to stop him screaming to Katie.

"Get in the truck! We are going for a ride," Roy said.

Joshua didn't move, hoping Roy wasn't strong enough to life him in, but he was. Roy lifted Joshua into the truck slid him over the passenger seat, took the keys from the door and drove the truck down into the woods.

They were just inside of the woods, where Roy pulled up the truck and opened the door. Joshua tried to slide out the other side.

“Don’t be stupid! Where do you think you are going to?” Roy laughed “You can’t even stand up.”

Roy tied Joshua’s hands together. Then with one swift strike, he hit Joshua with the rifle straight across the head, knocking him out. Roy tied a rope around Joshua’s good leg, hung him upside down and waited for Katie to find them. He sat on the ground.

So, do I use the knife or the gun to kill them? I’ll kill them both. I let dear, sweet Katie chose how he dies!

Chapter 42

Katie was on the phone with Barbara,

"Hello, Barbara!"

"Hello, Katie! Are you both okay?" Barbara asked.

"Yes. It's been quiet through the night, and Troy is on his way home," Katie said.

"How are you?"

"I am okay. So, how's Joshua coping?" Barbara asked.

"He's okay. He went out to get his phone, a little while ago. He's probably chatting to Bryan," Katie said.

"Katie! Joshua's not talking to Bryan! Bryan is standing right next to me, drinking tea."

"Really! Hold on a minute," Katie said, walking towards the door to check Joshua was still by the truck.

Katie gasped, "Barbara, I have to go!"

"Katie, what is going on?"

"The truck and Joshua are gone. I need to find him!" Katie said.

"Okay. Call me when you find him," Barbara said.

"I will," Katie said, before hanging up.

Katie was starting to feel the panic set in.

Where is he? What do I do now? I take the gun and baseball bat, and I will go and find him.

Katie ran down the corridor to the gun closet and pulled out a 260 Remington rifle. She slammed the door shut to the gun room and ran back to the living room.

I should call his phone first!

Katie dialed Joshua's number. The phone rang for what seemed like forever, and then someone picked up the phone,

"Joshua!" Katie said.

“Hello, sweetie! Joshua? So that’s his name! He can’t talk right now,” Roy said.

“Roy! What have you done? Where’s Joshua?”

“Oh, he’s hanging around somewhere, you know like an unpleasant smell!”

“What?”

“We’re in the woods. Why don’t you come join us, Katie?”

Katie dropped the phone, took Troy’s prize baseball from the wall and walked outside, with the rifle under her arm and the baseball bat in the other. She saw the blood on the ground where the truck had been parked.

Oh, Joshua! I guess it’s all to me now, time to deal with Roy once and for all and save Joshua. Funny, men are supposed to be so strong, and here I am trying to rescue one.

Katie made sure the gun was loaded. And continued into the woods, knowing there was no time to waste!

Chapter 43

Katie soon found Roy standing by a tree with a smug look on his face. She could see Joshua hanging from one leg dangling un-conscious, with a cut on his forehead.

“What have you done?” Katie asked.

“You’re pretty, when you’re angry! Have I ever told you that?” Roy asked.

“Roy! I am not playing games! Let him down now!”

“Well, no, I don’t think so!”

“What did you do to him?”

“Nothing, I just found him like this, but it is kind of amusing really. You seem very concerned about him!”

“You’re a psychopath.”

“I’ve been called worse, darling!” Roy said, taking a step toward Katie.

Katie raised the rifle and pointed it at Roy.

"Now, what are doing? Put the gun down, Katie. We both know you don't know how to use it. Even if you did you could never shoot me!"

Katie walked towards Roy slowly, one foot at a time, holding the rifle steady.

"Let him down, Roy!" she said.

"Then what, we all play happy ever after. No!" Roy said.

Katie moved neared again. Every time Katie step closer, Roy stepped back.

"Enough games, Katie, you can watch while I slit his throat."

"Not going to happen, Roy, you go near him, and I will shoot you myself!"

Roy took the hunting knife in his hand and turned toward Joshua. Katie shot a bullet straight into Roy's shoulder.

"For God's sake, Katie! Ouch" Roy cried.

"You need to leave us alone, Roy," Katie replied.

"I can't believe you shot me! But I have another arm, you know!

"Drop the knife, and step away from the tree."

"Or what? You'll shoot me again?"

"Yes actually!"

Roy took a step towards the tree. Katie shot another bullet into his shoulder.

"You always did like my shoulder," Roy said, stumbling backward.

Katie walked to the tree. She held the rifle in one hand, and she slowly lowered Joshua to the ground with the other hand.

"How touching that he's your main concern. But we are not done yet, Katie," Roy said.

Katie walked toward Roy with the rifle aimed at him.

“We are so done, Roy! It’s time to finish this,” Katie said.

Roy pulled out a gun slowly.

“Yes, let’s.”

Roy moved backward as Katie marched towards him with the rifle in her hands. Roy didn’t realize that, Katie was pushing him toward the cliff that overlooked the ravine. Katie had the rifle fixed on Roy as he moved backward and the baseball bat in her other hand. They were a few steps from the edge of the cliff. Katie stopped and steadied the rifle, curling her finger around the trigger. Roy raised his gun and aimed at Katie. Katie fired four times. Roy fell to his knees on the edge of the cliff. Katie lowered the rifle and walked toward him. Katie walked towards him, determined that she would end his behavior once. As she stood looking over him, he was bleeding. There was so much blood, but Katie didn’t care. The sight of his blood dripping out of his wounds didn’t make her feel sick or anything else.

“But Katie! I love you!” Roy said, expecting her to stop or at least pause.

“I hate you!” Katie said, as she swung the baseball bat, hitting Roy straight in the stomach. Blood splattered on the bat from his bullet wound, and the blow knocked Roy into the wild ravine below.

Chapter 44

Katie turned around and walked back toward Joshua. He was lying on the floor where she had left him. His leg was all bloody. Katie ripped the sleeve from her top, made a bandage and started wrapping it around Joshua's leg. Joshua was beginning to open his eye's.

"Katie!" Joshua whispered.

"Hey, sleepy head!" Katie replied.

"Roy? Where is he? He was here, Katie?"

"Shhh, he's gone!"

"Gone? Where?"

"Hell, hopefully. I took care of it," Katie said.

"What have you done Katie?" Joshua asked.

"I had to. He was going to slit your throat. I shot him!"

“How many times? I doubt you killed him if you shot him once.”

“Oh, I shot him a few times. Then I hit him with the bat, and he fell into the ravine. Trust me, Joshua: it’s over!” Katie said.

“Katie, remind me never to get on your bad side! We need to check the ravine, to make sure he’s dead!” Joshua said.

“You need to go to the hospital before that leg gets infected.”

“I am fine. Come on!” Joshua used the rifle to stand up.

“Okay! Then we are going to the hospital!”

Katie and Joshua slowly walked down the path to the ravine. The water was wild, but there was no sign of Roy anywhere. They searched up and down the ravine and looked at the rocks on the cliff to see if they could find him.

“Nothing so that’s it, right?” Katie asked.

"I guess so. The water must have washed him away," Joshua said.

They walked back to the truck. Katie helped Joshua in and drove it back to the lodge.

Katie helped Joshua inside and put a towel underneath him to catch any excess blood from his leg. Katie put the baseball down and took the rifle to check the lodge was secure.

"Everything is fine," Katie said, walking back into the living room.

"Okay. Isn't Troy's prized baseball bat, covered in Roy's blood? What are you going to tell Troy?" Joshua asked.

"I don't know. Let's get your leg sorted out first," Katie said.

Troy walked in.

"Katie! What is going on?" he asked.

"Troy! You're home," Katie replied.

"Hey, Troy!" Joshua said.

“Joshua!” Troy said.

“Well, Roy showed up and kidnapped, Joshua,” Katie said.

“Uh huh! Are you okay?” Troy said, looking at Joshua.

“Yeah, he stabbed me in the leg,” Joshua said, nodding at Troy.

“So, where is he now?”

“We don’t know we think he is dead somewhere!” Katie said.

“Katie shot him and pushed him over the cliff into the ravine!” Joshua said.

“You did what? Did, you check the ravine?” Troy asked.

“Yes. No sign of anything!” Katie replied.

“Okay! None of this explains why my prized, one-of-a-kind baseball bat is covered in blood though,” Troy said.

“Well, I kind of used it to knock Roy into the ravine. But I didn’t mean to ruin it. Sorry!” Katie said.

"All right. Let's get Joshua to the hospital then!" Troy said, helping Joshua up.

They all went to the hospital. while Joshua was being seen. Katie phoned Barbara.

Katie walked back into the treatment room and smiled at Joshua.

"I will just get his medication and notes done and he can go," the doctor said.

"Thank you." Katie said.

"You are going to be okay!" Katie said.

"I'm fine, don't worry," Joshua answered.

"I'll get stuff sorted so we can get out of here," Troy said leaving the room.

Katie leaned over and kissed Joshua.

"I love you!" Katie said.

"I love you, too!" Joshua replied.

The following morning Troy woke early. Katie and Joshua were still sleeping upstairs. Troy had slept downstairs in case Roy did show up, but also because he hated sleeping in the bed without Josie. He decided to go outside and clean the truck, so Joshua could return it to the rental company when they left. Roy looked at his lucky baseball bat as he walked out the door.

Well, the bat has had it. I don't know what possessed Katie to take that with her. Well, at least she put it to good use. I will have to start calling her bad ass Katie soon.

As Troy came in from cleaning the truck, Katie and Joshua were walking into the living room.

"Morning, you two!" Troy said.

"Morning, Troy!" Katie and Joshua said together.

"So, what plans do you have for today?"

"Well, I guess now that it's really over, we will consider going home!" Katie said.

"Okay! I said I would get Josie after you have gone home. She was enjoying herself in Vermillion," Troy said.

"I was hoping to see her before I left. Maybe next time?"

"Next time? You planning to beat someone else to death Katie?" Troy asked.

"Troy! I mean we could visit again," Katie replied.

Katie could feel her face burn with embarrassment.

"You are both welcome anytime. I could teach Josh to shoot," Troy said.

"I'd like that!" Joshua replied.

"I'll make some tea," Katie said.

Chapter 45

Later that day, Joshua and Katie were on a flight back to Texas.

“Feels good to be going home, doesn’t it?” Joshua said.

“Yes, I miss the ranch and my own bed,” Katie said.

“I know what you mean. I can’t wait to get back to work!”

“It will be a little while yet. You have to let that leg heal.”

“You worry too much. I’ll be fine.”

“Yeah, you think I worry too much, but wait until Barbara starts,” Katie said, laughing and shaking her head.

I am glad to be going home now that the whole situation with Roy is over. Now it is time to get Joshua better.

It was early the following day when they landed in Houston. Katie had to get assistance with the luggage as Joshua needed help walking, and so they went on a motorized cart used by the airport staff. The biggest smile spread across

Katie's face when she saw Barbara. There was a moment back in Meaford, thatshe didn't think she would see her again.

Barbara's smile dropped when she saw Joshua struggle to walk toward her. Katie had never seen Barbara angry, but she could the rage all over Barbara's face.

"What, did he do to you?" Barbara asked.

"I'm fine!" Joshua said.

"I'm going to get a wheel-chair!" Barbara said.

"I don't need one!" Joshua said.

"I told you that, you're not going back to work anytime soon, Josh," Katie said, laughing.

"Do something, Katie! She's worse than you!"

Katie laughed. "Now, I would if I could, which I doubt, but this is really amusing." she said.

Barbara returned with a wheelchair and helped Joshua into it.

"I can walk to the truck."

"No, you can't. Do as you're told for once," Barbara said.

Katie had put the luggage on a cart and was following Barbara to the truck, laughing and shaking her head the whole way. Barbara stopped and opened the truck door.

"I don't know what you're laughing at Katie. You are going to have to look after him, day and night, and get anything he wants," Barbara said.

"Me?" Katie asked.

"Yes, you!" Barbara said.

Katie put the luggage in the truck, got in and sat down.

Joshua was sat next to Barbara, shaking his head and rolling his eyes.

Maybe we should have stayed in Meaford. I think Barbara is going to mother me to death! But Katie at my beck and call could be interesting.

They were soon back at Barbara's house. Joshua was sat on the sofa with his leg up, drinking a cup of tea Katie had just made him. Bryan came in.

"You're back. What have you done to your leg?" Bryan asked.

Katie looked at Joshua.

"Bryan! It's fine. It looks worse than it is," Joshua said.

"What happened?"

"Bryan! drop it already!" Joshua said.

"Joshua!" Bryan said.

"I just need to get back to work, and I'll be fine," Joshua said.

"Work! No! Not for weeks!" Barbara said.

"Weeks! Barbara!" Joshua said.

"Oh! He's going to have a heart attack in a minute," Katie said.

Bryan quietly left.

"Barbara! Can I borrow the laptop?" Katie asked.

"Yes, there you go," Barbara said, passing it to Katie.

"What are you going to do?" Joshua asked.

"I'm going to save your life, again. Apparently, that's what I do now!" Katie laughed.

"How?"

"You'll see," Katie replied.

Barbara was busy making dinner, and Katie was engrossed in the laptop while Joshua watched television. Katie stuck her head up, and said,

"Right. It's sorted, Barbara!"

"What? What's sorted?" Barbara said.

“Well, Joshua can stay here tonight. I mean he can’t go home. For tomorrow, I have booked this house on the outskirts of Fort Kellna. We will go stay there for a week, maybe two. Joshua needs rest and you will drive him crazy. Plus, it’s near the hospital to get his dressing changed and checked on.”

“You just got back!” Barbara said.

“I know. But isn’t Joshua’s recovery more important right now?”

“Yes. I can’t argue with that. Is it me or are you unusually keen to spend time alone with Joshua?”

“Barbara!” Katie said.

“Yes. I notice Joshua isn’t putting up any resistance,” Barbara said.

“Hey! It’s Katie. Why would I argue!” Joshua said.

“Really! Josh!” Katie said.

“Since when did you call him Josh?” Barbara asked.

“Oh, enough talking. That’s the plan. Deal with it,” Katie said, marching off upstairs to get a cardigan.

Chapter 46

Later that day, Katie and Joshua arrived at the house that Katie had rented for the week. It was just on the outskirts of Fort Kellna and close to Houston. Katie had driven Barbara's truck to get them there. She parked the truck and helped Joshua out the truck. The house had a single-story and had a grey and cream exterior. There was a winding path that led to the front door under a v-shaped roof. There was perfectly kept grass with small plants bordering the path. Katie would have stayed in a trailer to get away from Barbara and Bryan though.

"Katie! It's lovely," Joshua said.

"Yes, it is. And best of all, no stairs!" Katie said. Helping Joshua up and down stairs was hard work.

They went inside, and Joshua sat down on the black leather sofa and put his leg up.

“I’ll make a drink, and then I will get the bags in,” Katie said, going into the kitchen to make tea.

Katie returned with the tea.

“So how long do we have this place for?” Joshua asked.

“A week, but we can extend it, if we need to. I thought we would see how you’re feeling,” Katie answered.

“Great!” Joshua said.

“I thought we could get a takeaway tonight, and I’ll go shopping for food tomorrow,” Katie said.

“Sounds good! I am just happy we can spend time alone together.”

“Me too! You rest while I go sort the bags out,” Katie said, giving Joshua a hug.

The following day, Katie was up early. Katie had a nightmare the night before, about shooting Roy. It made her relive the events in Meaford from her finding Roy and Joshua in the woods to Roy saying, "I love you," Katie had woken up in a cold sweat. She showered, changed, and came into the kitchen.

What did I think? I could kill him and just walk away like everything was fine? I had to do it he would have killed Joshua and me. I would do it again if I had to! I need to learn how to live with this. I can't tell anyone about it.

Joshua came into the kitchen.

"Are you okay?" Joshua asked.

"Oh. Morning Joshua, Yes I am fine," Katie said.

"You got up early! I just wondered."

"I am okay! Do you want coffee?"

Joshua approached Katie.

"Yes, please. Katie, you can admit that you are not okay! You have been through a lot. He was your husband, and you had to kill him. God knows it can't have been easy."

I can't talk about this right now!

"I did what I had to. I don't want to analyze it. In fact, I don't even what to think about it. It's over. You're okay that's all that matters," Katie said, passing Joshua his tea.

"I am going to sit down and drink this," Joshua said.

I don't understand. She has never shut me out like that before. Okay. She did for a while after Katherine was killed. But not like this. It must be affecting her: she's not nearly cold hearted-enough to be able to kill someone and not have it affect her!

Katie and Joshua drank their tea in silence. When she had finished Katie said,

"I need to go shopping for food. Is there anything you want me to get while I am out?"

"I could come with you!" Joshua said.

"I think it's best that you rest. I want you to get better."

"Okay. Well in that case Pop Tarts and cola!"

"Pop-Tarts and cola? Are you twelve?" Katie laughed, and shook her head.

"It's what I eat when I want to feel better," Joshua said.

"Okay, Pop-Tarts and cola it is! I'll be back soon," Katie said.

"So, am I getting a hug or a kiss anytime?"

"Yes, sorry!" Katie said, leaning over and kissing Joshua.

"Bye, Katie!"

"I'll be back soon," Katie said, as she walked out the front door.

Katie got in the truck and sighed,

I am so grateful to just finally be alone, so I can just breathe.

Katie drove straight to the store to do the food shopping. She had almost got everything, but she couldn't find the Pop-Tarts. It took a little while, but Katie found the Pop-Tarts.

Katie was soon back at the house putting the shopping away.

"Did you get everything you wanted?" Joshua asked.

"Yes. Thanks," Katie replied.

"Great!"

"Katie! Can we talk?" Joshua asked.

"About?" Katie asked.

"You! Me! Roy!"

"Joshua! Not this again!" Katie said, walking over to him and sitting down.

"Katie. I feel like you are shutting me out, and I don't understand," Joshua replied.

"I don't mean to, but we're not equal partners in this. I shot Roy, I pushed him of the cliff, and I did it alone! I need to deal with this. I'll be fine, but it's going to take time."

"Katie, maybe we are not equal! In the end, I wasn't much help. But we are in this together. You had to do it. He would of, killed us both."

"I know, you're right. How's your leg?"

"Still hurts. I think the swelling has finally stopped though!"

"We should go the hospital tomorrow and get the bandage changed," Katie said.

"Yes, but can we sit on the sofa and watch television for a while?" Joshua said.

"Of course."

The following day Katie and Joshua got up early and went to the hospital. They were in the treatment room.

"So, Mr. Garcia, would you like to tell me what happened?" the nurse asked.

"I had a hunting accident in Ontario and fell on a knife!" Joshua said.

"Okay, let's have a look," said the nurse.

The nurse slowly unwrapped the bandage from Joshua's leg.

"It's healing nicely. I'll just redress it. You were very lucky," she said.

The nurse put a fresh bandage on Joshua's leg.

"When will it be healed? I would like to go back to work soon!" Joshua asked.

"I would give it two weeks, but I returned to work," the nurse said.

"He's a workaholic!" Katie said.

"They all are round here, dear!" the nurse replied.

They were soon back at the house. It was a lovely day, so Joshua decided to lay in the garden, Katie made some lemonade and joined him.

"I love you Katie. I think more than you will ever know."

“I love you too. Joshua. I am really looking forward to just being together without all the Drama.”

“Me, too!”

They lay there on the grass all afternoon. It got dark, and the stars appeared. Katie made a wish on one of the stars.

I wish to feel this in love forever and to hold on to this memory in my heart forever!

“What are you thinking about?” Joshua asked.

“Nothing really. Just looking at the stars. We should get inside,” Katie said, getting up.

The next few days fly by, Katie and Joshua just spent time together in the house and garden, enjoying the peace and quiet. They decided to leave the house after a week and return home. Katie drove Joshua home.

“Are you sure you are going to be okay?” Katie asked, before kissing Joshua.

"I'll be fine. I'll call you later," Joshua said.

Katie left and went home to Barbara's house.

"Katie!" Barbara said.

"Miss me?" Katie teased.

"It's been too quiet!"

"Ah, okay!"

"Want a cup of tea?"

"Oh, yes, please!" Katie said Dropping her bag and sitting on the sofa."

"So, where's Joshua?" Barbara asked.

"I dropped him at home!" Katie replied.

"Here's the tea. Is everything ok?"

"Yes, everything is fine. It's just time to get back to normal!"

"Normal? I am not even sure 'normal' exists anymore!"

“You know what I mean! So, how are things with you. Barbara?”

“Okay, everything is okay. It’s good to have you home. Katie!”

“It’s good to be home.”

Later that day, Katie had unpacked and was reading on the sofa when Bryan came in.

“Hi, Barbara! Hi, Katie!” Bryan said.

“Hi Bryan!” Barbara said.

“Oh. Katie, Joshua asked if you could meet him at seven, down at the den by the river?” Bryan said.

“That’s a strange request, but yeah, sure!” Katie replied.

“What is he up to? Bryan?” Barbara asked.

“I have no idea. I was just asked the deliver the message!”

“Yeah, right!” Barbara said.

"Oh, Barbara, leave him be!" Katie said.

"Okay, well I have done everything, so I am off for the day!" Bryan said.

"Bye, Bryan!" Katie and Barbara said.

Katie went back to reading.

"Aren't you curious, what Joshua is up to?" Barbara asked.

"Not really. I'll find out at seven and it's four now!" Katie replied.

"I am!"

"I'll tell you all about it when I get back. Right now, I am going for a long bath."

Chapter 47

Katie was ready to go meet Joshua.

"Barbara! I'm going to see Josh!" Katie said.

"Okay, Have fun! See you later," Barbara replied.

Katie slowly walked down to the den.

I wonder what this all about! He should be resting that leg of his.

Finally, Katie reached the den. Joshua was stood outside.

God! He looks good.

Joshua wore his jeans and a tight khaki top, which seemed to emphasize every muscle in the top half of his body. He was smiling, and his eye's danced and sparkled with excitement.

"Hello, Katie!" he said.

"Hello, Josh!" Katie said.

As Joshua stepped to the side, the den was shining with light. Katie stepped inside. There was a hot pink, satin blanket on the ground in-between the tree stumps. The blanket held down with 30 candles. There were little rose quartz crystals hanging from the branches above the den. Joshua followed Katie inside.

Katie knelt on the blanket.

"Joshua! This is amazing!" Katie said.

"Oh, wait. I forgot something!" Joshua said, standing up.

Joshua took a container of pink glitter dust and sprinkled some over Katie.

"Nice touch!" Katie said.

"Thanks. I am glad you like it," Joshua said.

"I love it!" Katie said, leaning forward to kiss Joshua.

"I have something, I wanted to talk to you about!" Joshua said.

"You did all this just to talk to me?" Katie asked.

"Well, yes," Joshua replied.

"What's on your mind?" Katie asked.

"Well, In Ontario, at one point. I wasn't sure I would survive. All I want is you Katie! If you will let me, I just want to dedicate my life to making you as happy as you make me!"

"Joshua. You already make me happy every day. I don't know how I would have coped without you!"

"Katie, let me finish, I want you to marry me Katie! I never want to be apart from you again. We can have that beautiful simple life we both dream about," Joshua said.

"I would you know, I love you, you're everything to me. But I am still married to Roy. Technically. I am widow, but I am not sure how the law stands on this," Katie said, placing her hand gently on Joshua's cheek.

"Let's just get engaged. We can sort the legal stuff later. We can ask Barbara to help she is great with official stuff like that. The question is, do you want to get engaged to me?" Joshua asked.

"Yes Joshua! Let's do it."

Katie leaned in and kissed Joshua. She lingered because the kiss was so soft and passionate. When the kiss ended, Joshua said,

"I love you so much."

"I love you too!" Katie said, kissing him again.

When they had finished kissing, Joshua said.

"So, what type of ring do you what?"

"I don't want a ring. I want a barn!" Katie replied.

"A barn?"

"Yes, well preferably with a little house attached to it."

"You are completely crazy. Do you know that?"

"It has been mentioned."

Katie cuddled into Joshua and lay there for most of the evening before they put out the candles and Joshua went home, and Katie went back to the house.

Josh and I engaged! I couldn't have asked for a better evening; it just seems perfect!

"Hello, Katie!" Barbara said, when she walked in.

"Hello, Barbara! Do you want tea?" Katie replied.

"Yes, but tell me what happened. I am dying to know!"

"In a minute, let me make tea first."

"But Katie!"

"Your curiosity, will kill you one day!"

"Yeah, well. I am old I have to die sometime! Tell me,"

"Okay, you're like a big child," Katie said, sitting down.

Katie passed Barbara the tea.

"You're still stalling."

Katie laughed.

"I can tell it was good by the smile on your face," Barbara said.

"He asked me to get engaged!" Katie said.

"He did what! What did you say?"

"Yes!"

"Oh my! You and Josh are engaged! That must have been some trip to Canada!"

"Barbara! Don't say anything until he tells you okay!"

"Oh, Okay. You know I am going to smile like an idiot every time, I see him though."

"Barbara, you are so funny. You are worse than a child."

"Wow! This is huge!"

"Yeah, I know," Katie said, leaning back into the sofa while holding her cup of tea.

Chapter 48

Meanwhile, Joshua was in his parent's tidy kitchen. He sat at the old pine table with his parents, Lisa and Stephen. Lisa was tall and slim with golden blonde hair tied up in a ponytail. She also had delicate facial features that were considered very pretty. She looked a bit like a porcelain doll. Stephen was a medium height and very muscular. He was a rugged-looking man with brown hair and blue eyes.

"I need to tell you something," Joshua said.

"Okay!" Stephen said.

"I proposed to Katie tonight, and, well, she said, 'yes'."

"Joshua Garcia! You did what?" Lisa said.

"Katie Kyle with the nutcase of a husband that the town swore to protect her from?" Stephen asked.

"Yeah! Dad listen the husband is long gone. And, well, I love her," Joshua said.

"Joshua, this is crazy!" Lisa said.

"Mom, it's done. okay! You can either support me or not. I don't really care!"

Lisa stood up and walked to the kettle. "Fine!" she said.

"Your mother is complicated; you need to give her time to get used to the idea. Are you sure this is what you want?" Stephen said.

"It's all I ever wanted. She's everything I want dad!"

"Very well! Congratulations then. You have my full support!"

"It means a lot. Thanks," Joshua said, as he left the room.

"You're as crazy as he is Stephen!" Lisa said.

"Lisa, it's done. The way I see it is that you can support the boy or lose him which is it going to be love?"

"What if he gets hurt?" Lisa asked.

"More reason to support him so that we can help. Isn't that what families do?"

"Fine! You're right as always. Call him in here," Lisa said.

Stephen smiled. "I love you!" he said.

"Joshua, can you come down a minute?" Stephen shouted down the hall.

Joshua came in a few minutes later.

"Yes?"

"I...I am sorry, son, I was just in shock. So, did you give her a ring?"

"No, I didn't. No ring yet anyway," Joshua said, giving his mother a hug.

"Joshua! Who proposes with no ring? We raised you better than that. You will give her your grandmother's ring. Do you understand?" Lisa asked.

"Yes, Mom!" Joshua said, rolling his eyes.

As Joshua was leaving the room, his dad said,

"Like a said complicated!"

"Stephen! I can hear you. You know!" Lisa said.

Joshua laughed and shook his head as he left.

Chapter 49

It was early the following morning, and Barbara was in the kitchen preparing breakfast as usual when the telephone rang.

"Hello, Barbara! It's John," the voice said.

"Hello, John! What can I do for you?" Barbara asked.

"I heard Katie was back."

"That's right. Yes, she is! Is everything okay?"

"Yes, I have news from England, so I need to her."

"It's not bad news, I hope."

"Depends on how you look at it! Best you come with her, I think. So, when could you come in?"

"About ten. Is that okay?"

"Yes, that's great. See you then."

"Bye, John."

I wonder what can be going on. I mean they can't have found him, or it would be news from Canada!

Barbara went back to making breakfast. Katie smelled the coffee Barbara was making and came bouncing down the stairs.

"Morning, Barbara!" Katie said.

"Morning, Katie!" Barbara said.

Katie poured herself a coffee and sat down at the table.

"Katie, are you planning to go to work today? You looked dressed for the stables!"

"Yes, I am. That's why I got up early."

"I'm sorry, Katie. John just called. We have to go see him at ten. He has news for you from England," Barbara said.

"Okay, I will change, after breakfast. Did John say what the news was?" Katie asked.

"No, he didn't"

"Okay."

Katie ate breakfast and then went upstairs to get ready. When she came downstairs, they left for the police station.

They were at the local police station and John was walking towards them.

"Hello, Katie! Thank you for coming in. Hello, Barbara!" he said.

"Hello, John! What's this all about?Barbara asked.

"That's ok, What's it all about?" Katie asked.

"Let's sit down," he said.

"I had another call from the police in England. Last time they tracked his phone. Roy had returned to London. But since then, his phone has just disappeared, and no-one has heard from since or been able to track him. They think his phone was destroyed. They have exhausted all their resources and have no other choice but to presume Roy dead. Katie!" John said.

"I understand. So, do you really think he's gone?" Katie asked.

"I read the file and honestly, yes! I think something happened to him in London, and we will probably never know what."

"Thank you!" Katie said.

"Can I get you a cup of tea? This must be a shock!"

"I...I would rather just go home unless you need me for anything else," Katie said.

"No. That's all. Take care, Katie."

"I will. Bye, John!"

"Bye, Barbara!" John said.

"Good-bye, John!" Barbara replied, putting her arm around Katie as they left the police station.

Katie and Barbara drove home. When they got there Joshua was sat on the sofa. Katie sat on the sofa next to Joshua.

“What happened?” he asked.

“The English authorities are announcing that Roy is presumed dead!” Katie replied.

“That’s good, right? I mean, that means it’s over,” Joshua said.

“Yeah, it does,” Katie said.

Chapter 50

A week later, Joshua and Katie sat with Barbara at the table, eating lunch.

“So, engagement party!” Barbara said.

“What?” Katie replied.

“We never said, we wanted a party!” Joshua said.

“Oh, you’re having a party. I mean, no ring is one thing, but you have to have a party!” Barbara replied.

“Yeah, about the no ring thing!” Joshua said.

“What about it?” Katie asked.

“My mom is insisting you have my grandmother’s engagement ring,” Joshua said.

“Aww, how sweet!” Barbara said.

“Hello? Do I get any say in anything!” Katie asked.

"If you plan the party with me, you can have all the say, you want!" Barbara added.

"That's a good idea, Katie!" Joshua said.

At least if Katie helps plan it, she will keep it small!

"Okay. I'll help!" Katie said.

"Great! So, I was assuming you wanted something small. We can make a guest list!" Barbara said.

"If I am going to do this, I want a huge party. Like everyone we know. I know it's unlike me, but I love Josh so much I just want to celebrate in the biggest way possible with everyone. But where are we going to have it though. I was thinking maybe 300 hundred people should attend," Katie said.

"We can do that. We can use two fields down towards the bottom of the ranch," Barbara said.

"I am going to find Bryan. He must be on lunch by now," Joshua said, getting up and shaking his head before he left.

"I think we scared him!" Barbara said.

Katie laughed, "I am sure he's fine!"

Later, that day, Barbara and Katie got home from town, with food, Joshua was sat on the sofa with his leg up.

"Can you call Bryan to come up for dinner, we got food," Barbara said.

"Okay," Joshua said leaving the house to call Bryan.

Joshua had just taken his phone out his pocket, when he saw Bryan walking up the path towards him.

"Hey, Bryan! Barbara has got dinner in," Joshua said.

"Great," Bryan said.

"Yeah! You can save me from all this engagement party nonsense! They went to town and Katie all excited, too," Joshua said.

Bryan laughed. "Leave them to it. I am not getting involved in that," Bryan said, as he and Joshua walked back inside.

Barbara had laid all the food out on the table. There was salad, fried chicken, ham, cheese, slaw, potato salad, apple pie and lemonade.

"Looks great. I am starving!" Bryan said.

They all sat down to eat.

"This party is going to be amazing!" Barbara said.

"We need to set a date. Josh," Katie said.

"I don't care. It is up to you!" Joshua replied.

"A week from Saturday!"

"Why not? Sounds great!"

"Let's eat before Bryan eats everything," Barbara said.

They all laughed before eating dinner.

Chapter 50

The following days were filled with heavy activity. The invites had been sent out and Katie was glad that Troy and Josie had accepted and were flying in. Barbara was busy running around making sure everything was perfect. Bryan was running the ranch while all this was going on. Joshua was just keeping out of the way.

On the day of the party, Katie was laying out outfits on her bed. Katie's outfit was a plain, cream, pure- cotton skater dress, with little, light-pink heels ("like a Barbie doll,"Joshua had commented when she proudly showed them to him). Joshua's outfit was light blue jeans and a grey long-sleeve shirt. There was a photo shoot planned at six p.m. in the woods behind the ranch just before the party.

"Katie, it's time to go," Joshua called up the stairs.

"Okay, Joshua," she replied.

It was time to pick up Troy and Josie from the airport. Katie had arranged for them to stay at Barbara's.

"Ready? I don't what to be late!" Joshua said.

"Yes, we have plenty of time. Stop stressing," Katie said, following Joshua to the car.

They made it to the airport with plenty of time. They sat in the arrivals lounge and waited. Finally, Katie could see Josie walking towards her.

"Josie!" Katie shouted.

Joshua followed Katie. He saw Troy just behind Josie as she got nearer.

"Hey, Katie! Congrats, sweetie," Josie said.

"Troy!" Joshua said.

"Josh! How's the leg doing?" Troy asked.

"Yeah, it's good. Let's get out of here,"" Joshua replied.

"Hi, Troy! I am so happy you guys could make it!" Katie said.

"We wouldn't miss it for the world," Troy said, as they headed to the car.

They were soon all at Barbara's house.

"This is the ranch? It's huge!" Josie said.

Barbara was waiting in the doorway.

Katie and Josie walked towards Barbara with Troy and Joshua behind them.

"Barbara! This is Josie and Troy!" Katie said.

"Hello! Welcome!" Barbara said.

"Hi, Barbara!" Josie said, leaning forward to give Barbara a hug. And they all went inside.

Later than day Katie and Joshua came downstairs together.

"You look beautiful, Katie!" Troy said.

"She does!" Barbara said.

"We got to go. We will see you at the party," Joshua said.

"See you later!" Katie said.

"Bye!" they said.

Katie and Joshua walked into the woods to attend their engagement photo shoot. Katie rested in Joshua's arms, posing for the photos, and it was soon over and time to make their way to the party.

"Katie," Joshua said.

"Yes?" Katie replied.

"I love you! So much."

"I love you, too. Are you feeling nervous?"

"A little, but it's okay!"

"It's just another party, Josh!"

"Okay!"

They arrived at the field where the party was being held. They could see people still arriving as they walked towards the tent. There were two, huge, cotton fabric draped tents.

Inside, the tents were joined together. There was a drinks bar to the side of the tent on the left, and a present table on the right. There were lots of round tables draped in light grey table clothes with pastel pink napkins on the tables. Each table seated about eight people. There were dark wood and cream chairs around the table. There were huge centerpieces on each table. The tall and wide vases dripped with pink and creamhydrangeas, deep pink roses and crystals. There was a cake at the front of the tent on a table covered with a pink tablecloth. The cake was made of three tiers that were decorated with flowers up the side and on the top tier.

"Barbara did a great job. This is lovely!" Katie said.

"Yes, she did. It's something else!" Joshua said, kissing Katie.

Katie and Joshua went to sit down at one bigger table at the back of the tent. Troy, Josie, Lisa and Stephen were sat at this table.

Soon the tent was full of people. Everyone was seated. Barbara joined Katie at the table along with Bryan.

Barbara stood up to make a speech.

"Welcome everyone, to Katie and Joshua's engagement party. Their engagement came as a shock to us all, I think. But I couldn't think of two people more perfect for each other. I love them both dearly," Barbara said.

Everyone clapped. Soon after the food came out, and everyone was eating.

Katie looked at Joshua,

"Are you okay?" Joshua asked.

"Yeah, everything's perfect," Katie replied.

"So, how long of an engagement are you planning on?" Stephen asked.

"Quite long. Dad," Joshua replied.

Barbara laughed, while Katie just smiled.

After they had finished eating Katie went to talk to Cordy, Katelyn, and Lynette who were sitting near the entrance, and Joshua talked to Bryan.

"Katie, I can't believe how quiet you kept this!" Katelyn said.

"It was all very sudden, really," Katie replied.

"So, how did he propose? Was it very romantic?" Cordy asked.

"Erm, yeah it was down by the river. It was very pretty!"

"Cordy, Katie doesn't want to spill the details. Somethings should just be private!" Lynette said.

"Thanks, Lynette," Katie replied.

"We should all have a night out!" Cordy said.

"Yeah, I would be up for that! I am going to go find Josh. See you all later," Katie said.

Katie found Joshua stood near the table where they were sitting, still talking to Bryan.

“Hey, Bryan! Are you having fun?” Katie asked

“Yeah, I am so happy for you both. This party is great. Your friends, Troy and Josie are great!” Bryan said.

“Thank you,” Katie replied.

“Hey, Katie! Having fun?” Joshua asked, kissing her on the cheek.

“Yeah. It is lovely. Barbara is so good at parties.”

“Yeah, she has had a lot of practice!”

“So, Bryan how’s my horse been?” Katie asked.

“He’s okay. he kicked me the other day!” Bryan said.

“Really! I am coming back to work Monday!” Katie replied.

“Yeah, me too. If Barbara lets me,” Joshua said.

“She said something about light duties only!” Bryan said.

“What does that mean?”

"I think it means you get to walk around with a clipboard telling everyone what to do!" Bryan laughed.

Katie laughed, too. "So pretty much what he always does then," She said.

"Katie!" Joshua said.

"I'm sorry. I was only messing."

"Okay!"

"I think we should take a walk around, to talk to everyone. Then we announce we are going to the hotel Barbara booked for us."

"What hotel?" Joshua asked.

"It's in downtown Houston!"

"Okay, good!"

Chapter 51

A while later, Katie and Joshua were driving through downtown Houston looking for the hotel. Suddenly, Katie spotted a sign to go off the interstate. They were on a freeway which runs through downtown Houston.

"It's down there on the left, Joshua!" she said.

"Okay!" Joshua said, driving into the correct lane.

They were soon pulling up outside the hotel. It was a huge building made from mirrored glass. Joshua parked the car in the car park. As Katie and Joshua approached the entrance, Joshua was stunned at how sophisticated the hotel was the entrance was a small door with lights on either side with small conifers either side in wooden pots, A large grey welcome mat was placed outside. There were illuminated glass panels on either side of the door on the wall.

Inside there was a reception desk made from pine lacquered wood. There was a large painting above in and some purple flowers in a vase rested on it.

“Can I help you?” the desk assistant asked.

“Yes, we have a room booked under the name ‘Katie Maddison’,” Katie said.

“Yes, you booked the ‘Eternal Love Suite.’ Miss Maddison, please sign here,” the assistant said, passing Katie a book and pen.

Katie signed the book and passed it back.

“Breakfast is served between 7:30 – 10:30 AM. Have an enjoyable stay,” the assistant said, passing Katie a room key.

Joshua and Katie slowly made their way up to the room, which was on the eighth floor.

“This place is really fancy,” Joshua said.

“I know. It’s lovely!”

Joshua soon became stunned again when Katie opened the suite door. There was a king-sized bed with perfectly crisp white linen and a little bench at the end. There was a wooden and leather table, four chairs a beige corner sofa, and a flat screen TV. To the left of the TV was a marble worktop with a microwave and tea and coffee makers. In the corner, was a free standing, white bathtub.

Katie jumped on the sofa.

"This is great!" she said.

"I feel spoiled!" Joshua said.

"Come here, Joshua!" Katie said, pulling him closer to sit down with her.

Joshua sat next to Katie.

"Are you okay?" Katie said.

"Yeah, just a bit shell-shocked," Joshua said.

Katie leaned in and kissed Joshua slowly passionately. When she finished, he said,

“Keep doing that, and I will feel a lot better!”

“Okay!” Katie replied, kissing him again.

Katie lay down on the sofa and put her head on Joshua’s lap. Joshua started stroking her hair.

“Today has been great, don’t you think so?” Katie asked.

“Yeah! I have never been happier,” Joshua said.

“I’m glad. I love you so much.”

“I know, you keep telling me! Only kidding. I love you, too!”

Katie sat up and hit him with a cushion.

“Oh, you want a pillow fight!” Joshua said, kneeling on the sofa and hit Katie on the top of the head with a cushion.

Katie fell back laughing. “At, least you’re having fun now,” She said.

"I always have fun with you, Katie!"

"Good. I am going to have a bath and get changed," Katie said.

"Okay."

Katie suddenly realized the bath was in the middle of the room, and she would have to bathe in front of Joshua, so she took a shower in the bathroom instead. Katie reappeared from the bathroom in a long, pale-pink, silk nightgown with lace at the top.

"Wow!" Joshua said.

"What?" Katie asked.

"You look stunning. It amazes me how you look amazing in everything!"

"Thank you! It was getting late, so I thought I should get ready for bed."

Joshua walked towards Katie, pulled her close and slid his hands around her waist. Katie felt a hot flush running up her body like when a hot spring releases a burst of steam.

God! It's sexy when he does that. I think I blushed. I wondered if he noticed. I hope not!

Joshua kissed her. Katie didn't want him to stop, but she felt like she might fall over at any moment. Her legs were weak, but she just wanted Joshua to hold her.

"It's late. We should go to bed," she said.

"Okay," Joshua said.

I'm not sure if that's the invitation it seems to be! Joshua thought.

They climbed into bed, and Katie slowly cuddled up to Joshua and kissed him again. Joshua slid his arms around Katie. She felt the hot flush once more. Katie grasped the white cotton linen in her hands and pulled the blanket over them.

Printed in Great Britain
by Amazon